# Singulars
## A country of drugs and bullets

*A country of drugs and bullets*

| | |
|---|---|
| Chapter 01 | 4 |
| Chapter 02 | 11 |
| Chapter 03 | 15 |
| Chapter 04 | 17 |
| Chapter 05 | 21 |
| Chapter 06 | 23 |
| Chapter 07 | 27 |
| Chapter 08 | 33 |
| Chapter 09 | 36 |
| Chapter 10 | 42 |
| Chapter 11 | 46 |
| Chapter 12 | 48 |
| Chapter 13 | 51 |
| Chapter 14 | 55 |
| Chapter 15 | 57 |
| Chapter 16 | 60 |
| Chapter 17 | 62 |
| Chapter 18 | 66 |
| Chapter 19 | 70 |
| Chapter 20 | 74 |
| Chapter 21 | 76 |
| Chapter 22 | 78 |
| Chapter 23 | 81 |
| Chapter 24 | 87 |
| Chapter 25 | 90 |
| Chapter 26 | 92 |

*A country of drugs and bullets*

| | |
|---|---:|
| Chapter 27 | 99 |
| Chapter 28 | 103 |
| Chapter 29 | 106 |
| Chapter 30 | 109 |
| Chapter 31 | 113 |
| Chapter 32 | 116 |
| Chapter 33 | 119 |
| Chapter 34 | 123 |
| Chapter 35 | 126 |
| Chapter 36 | 131 |

*A country of drugs and bullets*

# Chapter 01

There is one truth in this world, history is written by the ones in power. Since ancient times all around the three continents, the center of history was in the hands of people with amazing abilities; those persons were called singulars. There are rumors that some of them had the power to control the land, to open the seas, some of them had strange bodies, with claws, wings or tails, others looked like regular humans but had supernatural strength or speed. Singulars were unique, extremely rare; they used their power for their own interest, to gain wealth, military and political power. Singulars fought other singulars to gain access to more resources and territory as a display of their greatness.

Singulars made alliances to fight stronger singulars, but every time a person in power was killed, thousands and even hundreds of thousands of humans died as well. Civilizations rose, kingdoms were born, and empires were created but most of them died. Until one day in the center of the old continent a man was born, a singular with unparalleled power.

Instead of conquering the world and leaving a trail of blood, He protected the weak unifying the humans, and with grace, nations voluntarily kneeled in his presence. Singulars ruled with fear, he ruled with hope. After his death his disciples continued with his will and started teaching his way of living, that continued for the next generations however some of them taught his life as philosophy, others as history and some as religion, everyone modified the facts according to their own agendas. War still exists but they are less frequent even though the last ones were the biggest.

There is peace in the world or at least an illusion of it, as the time passes, singulars become more and more common and the structure and rules of the game of power are changing. Soon the personal interests of the nations, the bloody history of the world and the will of the powerful will collide.

## *A country of drugs and bullets*

In the new continent, the country of Moon's navel, in the state of Snake Crawl it is a hot day in the deserted region of Tower city. Shaddai, a short red-haired young man with brown skin and green eyes, was walking down the streets, sweating but with a big smile on his face.

"God, I hate this weather, this country is so hot," Shaddai complained.

A skinny coyote the size of a bus walked nearby. Suddenly he stopped and sat under the shade of a candy tree to start licking the trunk.

"And the dogs are weird," thought Shaddai, looking at the giant coyote.

Shaddai continued to wander around, the streets were very lonely.

"I wish I could have taken the bus; I don't remember these streets."

The young man saw a couple over at the distance and ran to ask for help.

"Hey! Excuse me," he said.

Shaddai got closer and saw that the girl was against the wall and the man had a gun in his hand.

"Give me the purse or you're dead!" said the robber.

The girl was really scared hugging her purse.

"Excuse me, good sir," said Shaddai approaching the criminal.

## *A country of drugs and bullets*

The robber turned to point the gun at him, the girl was astonished.

"Do you know where River Street is? I want to visit a friend, but I am lost." Shaddai asked.

"Shut up and give me your money!" said the robber pointing the gun at Shaddai.

"I don't have any," he replied.

"Oh, you think you are being cute?" yelled the criminal.

The robber shot the gun, Shaddai dodged the bullets with a big smile and extended one of his hands at him.

"Sadness!" shouted Shaddai.

The robber dropped a tear, the gun fell from his hand, tears were raining from his eyes and finally, he fell on his knees and started crying out loud. Shaddai kicked the criminal in the head and sent him flying to the next block.

"Hey, you!" said Shaddai to the woman.

The girl was even more scared now and about to cry, Shaddai calmly smiled at her.

"Do you know where River Street is?" Shaddai asked nicely.

"Ye... Yes," said the woman.

Shaddai received instructions from the woman he just saved. After a few minutes, he arrived at a big green house, with a huge wall and steel doors.

"I didn't know Carlos lived near a bad neighborhood," thought Shaddai.

## *A country of drugs and bullets*

Shaddai knocked on the steel door and took a step back. After a few moments, a big muscled and bearded man opened the door, looked at Shaddai, and hit him hard, sending him across the street crushing the front wall.

"Phee," said the man.

Shaddai smiled, getting up from the debris.

"Hey Phee, Is Carlos there?" Shaddai asked.

"Phee," he answered.

Phee entered the house leaving the door open behind him, Shaddai entered as well.

"You know... You don't have to greet me like that every time," Shaddai added.

"Phee!" he shouted.

They both entered the house and Shaddai was greeted by a woman named Tisha. She was the mother of Carlos and Phee. Shaddai's friend's mom.

"Shaddai! Food is not ready yet, I am preparing your favorite dish," said Tisha.

"Yes!" said Shaddai, excited.

"Carlos is in the backyard. I know you have a special competition today." Tisha added.

"That's right! Today we'll settle our score." Shaddai answered.

"Phee!" Said Phee, mocking Shaddai.

## *A country of drugs and bullets*

Phee and Shaddai went to the backyard, a wide grass field, Carlos, a man in a wheelchair, was there. He was wearing a green armor with a lot of cables connected to it.

"99 wins in my favor 99 wins in yours," said Carlos.

"If I win, you'll have to go with me!" Shaddai replied happily.

"You better be ready to stay here then, have you decided the type of challenge?" Carlos asked.

"I am going with a good old-fashioned fight," Shaddai answered.

"You sure? Phee just finished my suit and since you can't use your singularity on me, you should choose another challenge." Carlos said confidently.

"Nah, I'll kick your butt anyway," Shaddai replied.

Phee, Carlos' older brother, was one of the best engineers in the country of Moon's navel. He had been working on a mechanic suit so his brother can move freely, however, Carlos is already powerful without it.

"Very well then," Carlos stated.

"Phee," Said Phee seriously.

"This Suit is not normal, it's powered by my singularity, my mental energy, so you won't be able to stall," Carlos warned his friend.

"Yeah, yeah, your brother is great, we all know that already," Shaddai said while stretching for the fight.

"Phee," Said Phee blushed.

### *A country of drugs and bullets*

"Either way I have a secret weapon as well, so let's fight already," Shaddai said, warning his rival.

Carlos and Shaddai stood against each other, Shaddai ran after Carlos and hit him with a double jab followed by a right straight. After that, he grabbed his opponent from the helmet with both hands and hit him with his knee. Shaddai threw a rain of punches over Carlos' suit then proceeded to kick Carlos on the chin and grabbed him from one of the legs and after spinning him around He threw Carlos through a wall. Carlos got up from the debris.

"This suit is lighter than steel and still way harder." Said Carlos while shaking the dust and pebbles on his suit.

Shaddai frowned. Carlos moved and hit Shaddai with a left punch followed by a right hook, finishing with a dropkick that sent Shaddai back. Both moved to the center of the backyard and exchanged blows.

"I think I am getting used to the suit."

"Shut up," Shaddai yelled.

Carlos landed a big punch on his rival and Shaddai felt on his back.

"Damn it, I am not hurting him nor tiring him." Shaddai thought.

Carlos did a hand a gun with his right index finger-pointing.

"Try this, Mental bullet," Carlos Exclaimed.

Carlos shot a green aura bullet from his finger and hit Shaddai.

"Phee, Phee, Phee," Phee laughed.

## *A country of drugs and bullets*

Carlos jumped over the wall to fight as a sniper and started shooting bullets at Shaddai, Carlos was inflicting a considerable amount of damage.

"Too bad I can't use my singularity against you, but I can still use it on me," Shaddai stated. Carlos kept shooting mental bullets, but every time he landed a shot, Shaddai laughed. Shaddai started laughing really loud. Carlos looked nervous under the helmet but kept shooting. Shaddai's body started glowing with a yellow light.

"Happy mode... HYPERACTIVE BODY," said Shaddai while glowing.

"Wha-"

Shaddai moved instantaneously behind Carlos and took him down from the wall with a big fast punch, Carlos was buried under the floor.

"Phee!" Phee exclaimed, shocked.

Carlos got up, Shaddai ran around Carlos hitting him at an incredible speed.

"This is bad," Carlos said to himself.

Shaddai threw a lot of punches to the suit and kicked Carlos on the helmet.

"HAPPY SHOTGUN," Shaddai shouted, finishing the combination with a powerful right straight blow. Carlos was sent flying, hit the floor, and made a big dust explosion. Shaddai went back to his normal state and Carlos was lying on the ground dirty.

"I win... so You will follow me to the old continent then."

*A country of drugs and bullets*

# Chapter 02

Carlos, Phee, Tisha and Shaddai gathered around the dinner table. Tisha cooked a juicy beef picadillo with potatoes, Shaddai's favorite dish. Tisha intended to comfort Shaddai with his favorite food since she thought he was going to lose the fight. Everyone was eating in silence, except Shaddai, he was quite happy.

"So, you will take Carlos with you?" Tisha asked.

"Well, that was the deal," Shaddai answered with his mouth full of food.

"Honestly, I thought this challenge was mine, as a psychologist I was excited to win so you could stay and have the opportunity to study your weird singularity." Said Carlos after drinking a sip of his glass of cola.

"I know I win, but I hate dragging people around. You don't have to follow me if you don't want to. I want you to come with me because you will be really helpful and the journey will be more fun that way," Shaddai added, giving Tisha some hope.

"You can come and visit us as much as You want Shaddai, you are part of the family," said Tisha.

## A country of drugs and bullets

"No mom, I gave my word, I lost, and I always had the intention of helping Shaddai one way or another. Besides if I follow you, I can learn a lot," Carlos stated.

"Phee," Phee added.

The family finished their meal and had a conversation afterward, they did some fun activities and Shaddai spent the night there while Carlos prepared for the journey. The next day both of them started their adventure.

Carlos and Shaddai started walking through tower city, another hot day as usual.

"So, which airport are we using?" Carlos asked.

"Airport? I didn't even have money for the bus on my way to your house" Shaddai said.

"You realize there is an entire ocean between the old and the new continent, right? We can't walk to it," Carlos said.

"I know, we are not going to the old continent just yet, we need to gather information about it first and I know the perfect person for that," Shaddai replied.

"Who?" Carlos questioned.

"My friend Hannah, she is an expert on the religion of the living God and therefore she knows a lot about the old continent especially the country of Amy. But we need a car for that," Shaddai answered.

"A car-" Carlos said but he was interrupted by a group of criminals.

"Well, well, it seems that these guys don't know whose territory this is." Said one of the thugs.

*A country of drugs and bullets*

"I know, there are a lot of criminals around here. They must be part of a big group. If we go to their base, we can borrow a car." Shaddai said with a big smile.

"Really? You want to "borrow" a car from the cartel?" Carlos complained.

"Hey, stop messing around and-" said one of the thugs before Shaddai hit him unconscious.

The group attacked Carlos and Shaddai, but they were easily handled. They didn't even need to use their singularities in battle.

"Ok, let's get the location of their base from them," Shaddai said.

"Are you... going to torture them?" Carlos asked with consternation.

"Not necessary, I can use my powers to make them say it."

The 2 friends got the information needed from the thugs, the base wasn't close, but it was near enough to go there walking in a couple of minutes. So, they decided to visit them and after a few minutes, they arrived at one of the city points of the cartel. Shaddai kicked the front door, destroying it.

"Carlos, back up," Said Shaddai.

The base had a huge garage at the center with several floors on the sides, the floors were filled with snipers, all of them aimed and shot the intruders.

"Mental shield!" said Carlos, creating a green aura roof to cover Shaddai and himself from the bullets.

*A country of drugs and bullets*

"Sadness!" exclaimed Shaddai lifting his arms and making the snipers fell in tears.

"I am sorry for the inconvenience, but may I take one of your vehicles please?" Shaddai asked politely and laughed.

From the main building, a tall purple-haired woman with light clothes and a whip came out. She looked at her surroundings and saw Carlos and Shaddai on top of the fallen gates.

"Why is everyone crying? What are you guys doing? Go and kill them," said the lady, whipping her men.

Carlos and Shaddai fought the men, one shooting everyone. The lady disappeared in the middle of the fight.

"Miss Aurora, why did you abandon us?" Cried out one of the defeated men.

Suddenly Aurora, the chief of the point, came out with an armored mechanical suit with machine guns as hands.

"Me abandoning my men?" I'll show you why not even the police mess around with us.

"Look Carlos is a suit like yours," said Shaddai laughing.

"Don't compare the work of my brother with that piece of garbage," said Carlos annoyed before hitting the enemy and ripping one of the machine guns.

Aurora attempted to shoot Carlos, but his suit was bulletproof. Shaddai started glowing and entered happy mode to attack the chief of the criminals.

"Hyperactive body," Shaddai said and then ran towards Aurora throwing a fast rain of jabs all over the mechanical suit.

*A country of drugs and bullets*

"Merry bullets," said Shaddai naming his attack before destroying the enemy's suit creating an explosion that ejected Aurora leaving her unconscious.

"Can I have a car now?" said Shaddai in the middle of a group of defeated grown men crying.

# Chapter 03

Carlos and Shaddai stood victorious, a man crawled towards them crying, Carlos aimed at him preparing himself to shoot him, the man grabbed Carlos from his foot.

"Please, help me escape, I am here against my will."

Carlos and Shaddai looked at each other, other members of the point started yelling the same thing.

"Where is their honor? I bet they just want to survive, it's probable that the upper ranks of the cartel will dispose of them because of this defeat and now they want to survive," Carlos Said.

"What if they are telling the truth and the cartel used them against their will? Well, it's not like they can lie to me, I am going to use that again" - Shaddai pointed at them with his hands - "happiness."

The men started to laugh uncontrollably then proceeded to say their true intentions out loud.

" Idiot, you really think we will betray our family. You are lucky the head of state is not here!" The man said.

## *A country of drugs and bullets*

"Told you," said Carlos, everyone was lying except one man that was laughing and couldn't talk.

"Help, the cartel killed my family and they made me work for them as a slave," said the guy laughing with tears dropping from his face.

"Jeez, I often forget how scary your singularity can be," Carlos added.

Shaddai approached the man, making him stop laughing.

"I am sorry for making you laugh while remembering that I will help you escape if you help us find a car."

Carlos covered Shaddai and his new ally while they searched for a vehicle, after a few minutes they found the keys for a big white pickup truck without plates.

"My name is Shaddai, and the metal man is Carlos, What's your name?"

"I am Juan, thanks for sparing me, here is the truck," replied Juan.

"You don't seem so happy; do you want me to make you laugh again?" Shaddai asked.

"No, it's just that after laughing and crying I am kind of exhausted," Juan replied.

"You are worried, aren't you? Even if you can walk free now, you feel like somebody's looking for you," Carlos said, and Juan remained silent.

"Do any of you know how to get to Tequila Lagoon?" Shaddai asked, interrupting Carlos and Juan.

*A country of drugs and bullets*

"No, are you telling me you don't know where we're going?" Carlos replied.

"Well, I know I need to go to Riverstone and that city is located in Tequila lagoon, but I am not familiar with the states of this place," Shaddai answered.

"I do, I know how to get to Riverstone," Juan added.

"It's settled then, you will drive us there and we will protect you from the cartel in return, how about that? You will join our journey."

# Chapter 04

Juan, Carlos and Shaddai were driving a big white truck in awkward silence. Carlos turned on the radio.

"The caravan of immigrants is approaching the southern border of the country, it seems like their true intentions are to cross Moon's navel to arrive at Eagle's nest and search for a decent life," said the man on the radio.

"I wonder how the president will react to this and more importantly, how people will react," said Shaddai reacting to the news and breaking the silence.

"Are you from Eagle's Nest?" Juan asked.

"That is correct, from Hogsfield to be exact."

"So, what are you doing here?" Juan asked.

"Well, I have family and friends in this country, well I should say that I used to have family in this country all of them are dead, presumably killed by the cartel," Shaddai answered.

## *A country of drugs and bullets*

"I get it, so that is why you are fighting these people, but if you want my advice, you shouldn't pursue revenge, I get that you 2 are singulars, you guys are strong, but Aurora was just a point leader, almost every regional chief is a singular like you, and even if you are able to defeat them, the state bosses are monsters, there is no chance you'll be able to fight them, so avoid getting their attention," Juan explained.

"Not to mention the head of the cartel, Chopo, he is the most wanted man, the last city he visited became the most dangerous in the country," added Carlos.

"Well, it's not like I want to dismantle the cartel, I don't care about the problems of this country, besides, even if the cartel was responsible, I have my reasons to think that another group was the mind behind the crime. In other words, don't sweat it, I don't have intentions to fight them unless they are in my way," Shaddai replied.

"Another group? Who do you think is responsible?" Carlos asked.

"The government of moon's navel," Shaddai said.

Juan was surprised and a little scared, but he focused on driving carefully, since the truck didn't have plates, he didn't want to grab the police's attention, then he noticed how Shaddai was always smiling and thought it was weird.

"Sorry, I have to ask, but I noticed that you didn't look worried or sad while talking about what happened to your family. Is this related to your powers?" asked Juan

"That is correct, I can make people happy including myself, I can also enhance the effects of those emotions."

"Wow, that is incredible, the ability to be happy whenever you want, I wish I had your singularity or any singularity, to be honest."

## *A country of drugs and bullets*

Carlos and Shaddai stayed quiet. The group was about to exit Tower city but just before they could enter the highway they were blocked by the police.

"Stop and get out of the vehicle that truck has been reported as stolen," Yelled the police officer using a megaphone.

Juan parked the car, he was scared, Shaddai got out of the truck.

"The other 2, get out of the vehicle as well, or we will shoot," said the other police officer aiming his gun.

"It's okay, I can handle it by myself," Shaddai said to Carlos and Juan.

"Now, this situation seems a little suspicious to me, this car has been used by the cartel, so I don't think they reported it as stolen, and you are threatening us even if you don't know if the car was stolen?" Shaddai questioned the officers.

"What the hell is he doing?" Juan exclaimed.

"This truck was reported a few months ago, we just found it today and besides you are trying to exit the city without plates, so we will take you with us."

"Correction, I am not trying to exit the city, I will exit the city, and let me know if I am getting it right, You are not asking us for a driver's license nor a registration or any other proof of ownership, instead you want to shoot us and take us with you, seems to me that you were blind when the cartel used this truck but you are really good detectives when we are using this truck," Shaddai replied.

"I hate smart mouths like you," one of the officers said.

The policemen shot aiming at Shaddai, but the happy man dodged the bullets and approached them kicking one of the officers in the jaw sending him away, then grabbed the other policeman by the neck and strangled him.

"I really don't like corrupt officers," said Shaddai with a creepy smile before throwing the man next to the road.

Shaddai walked towards the police car and kicked it to move it away from the road. Then he got in the truck and resumed their journey towards Tequila lagoon.

The kicked policeman was unconscious on the ground with a bloody face and the strangled officer was barely alive but with enough strength to take his radio.

"We were unable to capture them," said the officer with difficulty.

That report went to none other than the regional chief from the cartel of tower city. Every city that is part of the cartel territory has 1 or 2 regional chiefs that are overseen by the state boss. Eventually one of the regional chiefs of tower city had to report the defeat of Aurora and her point.

The regional chiefs from the state of snake crawl were having a meeting with their state boss, a bald, tall, muscled man with a huge scar around his neck.

"Well in my territory Aurora was defeated, all her men were annihilated, and the police were unable to stop them for us, so they are out of the city," said Orange, a tall skinny man with orange clothing and also one of the regional chiefs of tower city.

"Who will be so stupid to touch aurora or any of our men knowing that we are the chiefs," said Koko a gorilla man.

*A country of drugs and bullets*

"That's where things get interesting, all of our men were laying down crying, and the report said that 3 men were responsible, one of them a brown man with green eyes and red hair," Orange said.

Chuck, the state boss started laughing, and Koko and Orange laughed as well, leaving the other regional chiefs confused.

"So Shaddai is in the country and paid us a visit" - said Chuck laughing- "don't worry about it everyone, I'll take care of that myself."

# Chapter 05

The sky was dark, and a bright and beautiful full moon brightens the road in which the white truck without plates travels.

"Are we there yet?" asked Shaddai impatiently

"No, stop asking," said Juan tired.

"Being a member of the cartel doesn't seem like a bad idea now does it?" Carlos asked sarcastically.

"We still have some hours left, Riverstone is quite far from tower city, maybe we should stop and rest in a hotel," Juan suggested.

"That would be a great idea if only we had some money," Carlos replied.

"Where is your spirit of adventure? We are so close, and I am really excited to see my friend." Said Shaddai loudly and excitedly.

"My spirit of adventure died when you asked for the thousandth time if we were close to Riverstone," Juan answered frustrated.

"Well, are we? Are we there yet?" Shaddai asked... Again.

*A country of drugs and bullets*

"NO!" Carlos and Juan yelled.

"And what if we run out of gas, we are broke," Juan questioned.

"We walk," Shaddai answered.

"What do you mean We're broke? Aren't you supposed to be a criminal? I thought cartel members were rich," Carlos added

"Well, I am about to kill you both so, yes. I am a criminal, a broke one," Juan said.

"Maybe there is some money in this truck," Shaddai suggested.

"Or drugs," Carlos added.

"Do you really think the cartel is that dumb? You seriously think they would leave a dollar unprotected?" -Shaddai opened the glove box and found a couple of stacks of money - "they left money in this truck?" Juan asked.

"Well, would you look at that," Carlos said pedantically

"WE ARE RICH," Shaddai shouted.

"I hate you, I hate you both," Juan said through his teeth.

"Let's find a nice restaurant," Shaddai suggested with a glow in his eyes.

"And a hotel," Carlos added.

"Ok, sounds great," said Juan, changing lanes to get to the next exit of the highway.

# Chapter 06

Carlos, Juan and Shaddai entered the nearest city, Flaming Pond, in the state of Blistering Waters, a place well known for its food and thermal waters. The main street was lightened by the business signs and building lights, it was an energetic scene.

"There, let's stop and eat in that place," said Shaddai with confidence in his eyes.

"A buffet? There are a lot of places, we can go somewhere else," Juan said.

"This place is known for its food you know? we should try a local food truck," Carlos suggested.

"I am sorry, I didn't know I was surrounded by cowards. All you can eat, it's challenging us," Shaddai replied excitedly.

"It's not like that, it's not a challenge," Juan added.

"All buffets are challenges, and I won't back down," said a hungry Shaddai. They parked the truck in front of the restaurant and stretched before entering the building.

"What do you think about making this our next duel Carlos?" Shaddai said.

*A country of drugs and bullets*

"First of all, it is my turn to choose the challenge, second I am not crazy enough to challenge you in a food competition," Carlos replied.

"I'll challenge you Shaddai, I'm so hungry that I could eat a cow," said Juan.

"Just one?" Shaddai asked.

"Suit yourself," Carlos added, and the group entered the restaurant. Carlos took a small plate and a cup of coffee and sat at one of the tables. After a while Juan arrived with a big plate full of food and a big glass of lemonade, just after Juan sat at the table Shaddai arrived with a whole cake, Juan was impressed, Shaddai then devoured half of the cake in just one bite. Juan's face turned white; at that moment he knew there was no chance of winning.

"Told you," Carlos said. The three of them kept eating and having a nice conversation, sharing some jokes, some laughs, Shaddai looked like a balloon after eating half of the food in the restaurant. The owner wasn't pleased, Juan was genuinely enjoying himself for the first time in years. They left the buffet.

"Please never come back!" shouted the owner.

"It was a good idea that we stopped here instead of a food truck we could've ruined a small business," Juan said.

"Or we could give them the night of their business year," Carlos added, Juan entered the truck and Shaddai climbed to the trunk and laid down since he could barely fit in the front. Juan drove searching for a hotel, Carlos chose this time.

They entered the hotel and Carlos stopped at the lobby since he was the one with the proper documents, they got a big room.

## *A country of drugs and bullets*

"I will sleep now, I am really tired, this is just the second day I've been using the suit and after using it for the whole day I am quite exhausted," stated Carlos.

"Quite exhausted," Juan said laughing and mocking Carlos' vocabulary, but they all went to sleep, however, Juan was having some troubles and after rolling in bed for a while, he got out of it and noticed that Shaddai wasn't in the room.

Juan exited the room and went to the pool area of the hotel even though it was supposed to be closed, Shaddai was there.

"Having trouble sleeping?" Juan asked.

"I suffer from insomnia, so I am always having trouble sleeping."

"Well, I wasn't able to sleep either," Juan said and noticed that Shaddai wasn't smiling as usual.

"Are you ok?" Juan asked.

"Yes, I am just tired, like Carlos I used my singularity too much today," Shaddai explained.

"You did defeat a whole cartel point and beat those cops," Juan added.

"No, that was a piece of cake, I often use my singularity on myself, but people don't notice," Shaddai explained.

"I see that's why you are always so annoying, I mean happy," Juan said but Shaddai remained quiet. "It was just a joke I was trying to lighten the mood."

"I know, thanks for caring," said Shaddai but he seemed like a completely different person.

"Hey, why do you want to go to Tequila Lagoon?" Juan asked.

"I am searching for a friend; she has information I need before my expedition to the old continent. Well, the real reason is that I want her to join me, she is strong," Shaddai answered.

"And why do you want to go to the old continent?" Juan asked.

"Is the continent with the oldest history, the longest war is still being fought in that place and the central base of the universal church is there, what I am trying to say is that there is a reason to all that, I want to find the origins and truths about singularities," Shaddai answered leaving Juan speechless. "My theory is that singularities and the religions that worship the living god are somehow connected," Shaddai added.

"I believe that as well," Juan replied, impressing Shaddai.

"How so?"

"It's not a secret that the cartel and the government of this country are allies, you were right in suspecting them, but what a lot of people don't know is that the universal church is involved as well," Juan answered, Shaddai was astonished.

"How much do you know about this?" Shaddai questioned.

"Not much, it seems like the government is the bridge between the cartel and the church, supposedly they have these meetings, and they have a super-secret ritual called "the blessing" in them, that's why nobody dares to leave the cartel, they won't risk exposing those secrets, that's why I am a target now," Juan explained with a sad tone in his voice.

"I see, thanks for the information, it is really helpful."

*A country of drugs and bullets*

"I thought going after the cartel was dangerous, but your goal might uncover the secrets of the United Nations and the universal church, you might piss the strongest people on the planet," Juan added.

"Well, I am willing to bet my life on this adventure," said Shaddai with a sincere smile.

"Ok, it's late, and I have to take you to your friend, let's try to get some rest," Juan said.

# Chapter 07

"Are we there yet? Are we there yet? Are we there yet?" Shaddai asked without stopping.

"As a matter of fact, we are very close, we are already in the state of Tequila Lagoon, so Riverstone should be around the corner," Juan replied in anger.

"So, tell me about this Hannah girl, how is she, besides religious?" Carlos asked.

"I wouldn't call her religious, more like a girl with a spiritual lifestyle, at least that's what she says," Shaddai replied.

"She is totally religious," Carlos said.

"Say that to her face, it'll be your funeral," Shaddai replied.

"Is she hot?" Juan asked, trying to picture her in his mind.

"Well, she is blonde and has blue eyes," Shaddai added.

*A country of drugs and bullets*

"Oh, that's right she is from the Eagle Nest, I forgot since you don't look like you are from the Eagle Nest," Juan added.

"How am I supposed to look? Like a cheeseburger?" said Shaddai, a little annoyed.

"Oh boy, is she fat?" Juan asked, alarmed.

"I mean she is soft, wait, why will that matter?" Shaddai questioned, completely annoyed.

"We arrived," Carlos announced. The truck kept moving along the main street, the city was full of tall colorful buildings, the roads were made of stone, Juan drove all the way to the center so they could walk and search.

Shaddai was amazed by the beauty, the colors, and the smell of the city, people happily walking in the park, brown shiny rivers all around the places, and the weather was nice, something Shaddai missed, the streets were covered by the shadows of clouds and trees.

"It smells great, like wet stone, and meat," Shaddai said, taking a deep breath with a big smile.

"This is one of the biggest cities in Moon's navel," Carlos said.

Shaddai's jaw dropped, his eyes opened wide, and he yelled with excitement, "Is that? Is that? Real?" - Shaddai questioned, astonished looking at a bunch of tall trees full of tacos. - "a taco tree?!" Shaddai ran and climbed one of the taco trees to eat, "Holy guacamole! This is amazing."

"Is this the first time he sees a taco tree?" Juan asked, mocking Shaddai's behavior.
"Why is that river brown? Is it an apple juice river?" Shaddai wondered while climbing down, he took a sip from the brown river.

*A country of drugs and bullets*

"Shaddai no!" - Carlos warned, but it was too late, Shaddai spat all the liquid - "It's a tequila river."

"You don't like tequila man?" Juan said, looking at Shaddai with disgust.

"You should have warned me," Shaddai complained.

"The state is literally named Tequila Lagoon," -Carlos scolded his friend. - "Now what? Where is Hannah?"

"Hannah? I don't know, that's why we are here, to find my friend so she can tell me where to find Hannah," Shaddai answered.

"Wait a minute, Hannah is not here? Why did you make me drive to this place then?" Juan demanded.

"I already told you, to find my other friend."

"What if your friend doesn't know where Hannah is?" Carlos asked frustrated.

"She knows and if she doesn't, she can find out for us, and in the worst-case scenario we can fly to the old continent with the money we have," Shaddai answered while looking at the taco trees.

"So where is your other friend?" Carlos questioned at the edge of his patience.

"That's easy, she has a chocolate store somewhere in this city," Shaddai answered with confidence.

"This city is huge! We are not going to find it!" Juan yelled.

*A country of drugs and bullets*

"Maybe we can ask someone," -Shaddai said, and Carlos and Juan looked at each other. - "Excuse me, do you know where the Panda chocolate store is?" Shaddai asked a random person that walked by.

"Yes, everybody knows that store, it's pretty famous, you guys must be tourists, you'll just have to walk 3 blocks down the next street, and you'll find it," said the lady.

"Could you tell us how the store is?" Carlos asked, concerned.

"Oh don't worry, you will know which building is the store you are looking for," said the lady with a smile, she waved and kept walking.

"See, there is nothing to worry about," said Shaddai, laughing. "I hate you so much," Juan replied, and the group walked the 3 blocks in the direction they were told and there it was, a building with the shape of a panda's bear head.

"Let's go," Shaddai said excited and started running crossing the street, the other 2 followed him, Shaddai opened the door and entered, the store was full of customers and a woman with black short hair, meaty red lips and big eyes protected by glasses was serving drinks and chocolates.

"Honey? What are you doing here" said the young woman amazed.

"Cupcake! Long time no see," Shaddai replied, Juan was astonished by Cupcake's beauty.

"Cupcake?" Carlos thought.

"Please, sit, I'll be with you in a minute, candies," Cupcake said while carrying some dessert trays. The group sat down and waited, after a few minutes Cupcake brought a little metal car full of big fudge-covered brownies with chocolate chips on top and filled with homemade hazelnut spread.

"These are for Honey, what can I get for you Marzipans?" Cupcake asked.

"Just a coffee," Carlos said.

"Whatever you want," Juan said without taking his eyes from Cupcake.

"Sure thing caramel," Cupcake said and left.

"She called me caramel!" Juan said excitedly.
"If you don't stop being creepy, I'll beat you up," Shaddai said while eating a brownie.

"Since when are you nice to… you know, anyone?" Carlos asked Shaddai.

"What do you mean?"

"Cupcake? What is that about?" Carlos questioned.

"That's her name," Shaddai answered with the mouth full leaving his friends staggered.

"Here you go, here is your coffee, watermelon, I also brought a slice of dark chocolate cake," Cupcake said and served the same for Juan.

"So, what brings you here honey?" Cupcake sat down with them and asked Shaddai after finishing all of those brownies.

"I am searching for Hannah, I heard she was on a mission in this country, I was wondering if you had any information on her

*A country of drugs and bullets*

whereabouts," Shaddai answered, licking his fingers. Cupcake's face changed, she looked annoyed.

"Of course, you are here for her, and yes, she is in the country, all those eagle nesters with their savior complex love to do missionary work, but they never actually help, and sadly...I do know her location honey," Cupcake replied with a mean look that scared Juan and Carlos.

"Why is that sad? You will be able to help me," Shaddai said with a big smile.

"You can control emotions, but you are unable to read and understand them, honey," - said Cupcake, staring at Shaddai's eyes.

"She is in Crosstruth, nursing the community of Beauty beach. Now that I think of it, maybe she is helping a little, but now that you are here, you might want to stay at least for a couple of days honey," said Cupcake with some jealousy in her eyes.

"Well, if I can eat some of your food, I'll stay a little longer, your store is really cool," Shaddai replied, and Cupcake blushed and covered her face embarrassed.

"Stop it, you little marshmallow," said Cupcake, hitting Shaddai on the face.

"What is wrong with you?" Shaddai said laughing, Juan and Carlos were really confused by their dynamic.

"You might want to stay longer because the highest priest of the universal church is visiting Moon's Navel in a couple of days, he will be in this very city."

# Chapter 08

A couple of days have passed, Riverstone had been preparing to receive the highest priest, the government ordered the construction of a big and luxurious platform made entirely of gold in the middle of a big plaza of the city; people from all around the country and even from other countries gathered to hear the words of the universal church's leader, in the middle of the multitude, Shaddai, Cupcake, Carlos and Juan.

When the time came important people showed up like the city's mayor, the governor, the president of Moon's navel Henrick Pine, And from Seersong, home of the universal church in the old continent, the highest priest Benedict Paul XV and his most trusted men.

Shaddai had a serious face and was quietly sitting, he couldn't take his eyes out of the people on the golden platform. There was a dark and mischievous aura coming from Benedict Paul XV, but still, people watched him with sparkles on their eyes cheering and bowing before him. Carlos sat there observing the delicate ornaments of the place thinking of the insane amount of money the government should've spent on the event.

## *A country of drugs and bullets*

"My dear loyal and trustworthy sons of Moon's navel, it is with immense joy that I think of your perseverance in the ways of God, I am convinced that the people gathered here are devoted servants of the lord and the church, your prayers will be heard, and times of fruition will arrive at your habitations," said the highest priest, an old, wrinkled man.

"It's really eloquent and fluent for a person that speaks 15 languages," said Cupcake to Shaddai murmuring.

"However, I am aware that you face the dangers of sin, this country is under siege by the kingdom of darkness, do not let the devil enter your homes, do not abandon your faith which is your greatest weapon in these times," said the old man continuing his speech, Juan was nauseated by the words he heard.

"Afraid not, because the day will arrive in which you all be able to eat in peace and walk without remorse, I pray to god, send your light, open our ears to your words so we all can run to your presence with righteous steps, send your angels to combat the devils that torment the people of this country and the world, I here seal my petitions with the king's ring and the authority you have given me."

People clapped and praised, some of them cried while praying, the people of Moon's navel have been motivated and persuaded, however, there was one person listening on the top of a tall building, a blonde woman with dark clothes, milky soft skin, and long legs, a sword in a scabbard tied to her waist, and long white feathered wings on her back.

"You will regret saying those prayers Benedict," said Myrael, the mysterious woman.

The ceremony ended and people tried to push their way onto the platform wanting to at least touch the clothes of the highest priest; Shaddai stood on the top of a chair to take a look at the platform and

## *A country of drugs and bullets*

exchange glances with Henrick Pine, the group returned to the Panda chocolate store.

"I can't believe these people, they come to preach about the dangers of this country, dangers they create," Juan said, angry.

"The government sells its people to the cartel creating danger, then brings the church to those living in fear, the church gains followers and the president keeps the trust of the voters, it's a win-win situation for everyone." Carlos vented.

"Thank you Cupcake, it was an interesting event, I never have felt so many negative emotions inside of a person like with the highest priest, he is definitely not a server of any god nor a weak old man, and the president of this country did you notice his eyes?" Shaddai asked.

"I mean he is really handsome," Cupcake said.

"That's not what I meant, he has reptile-like eyes," said Shaddai excitedly.

"No, he doesn't," Cupcake replied.

"When we exchanged glances, I noticed he changed his eyes, like a reptile," Shaddai said trying to convince everyone. After discussing the event, the group thanked Cupcake and said goodbye.

"Thanks again Cupcake, I will visit you again when I come back from the old continent," Shaddai said merrily. The group now drives their white truck to Crosstruth in order to find Hannah.

# Chapter 09

After a bunch of hours driving, the group arrived at Crosstruth, to the popular city of Beauty beach, named after the beautiful women of the region; it is said that the colonizers of Moon's Navel were astonished by the women that received them the first time they arrived; it was warm and wet, Shaddai was already complaining, they had to drive through a big jungle full of life, colorful parrots, giant anteaters, leaf-like insects, and dangerous felines.

"I will have to park here; this city is occupied by the cartel. We don't want to draw any attention," Juan said, worried.

They parked the truck on top of a hill near the jungle on the outside of the city, so they had to walk.

"Now that I am more used to this suit, and have experience walking, I can formulate an opinion, walking sucks, it's overrated," Carlos said and Shaddai laughed. After walking for a few minutes, they encountered a group of kids playing some sort of tag game.

"No, I want to be the cartel and you will be the police," said one of the children playing.

## *A country of drugs and bullets*

"Oh man, cops suck, they are boring," said the other kid whining, the group of kids grabbed Shaddai's attention.

"Why would you like to be the cartel?" Shaddai asked, approaching the kids.

"Well, they are strong, they can do whatever they want," said the kid that appeared to be the leader of the children, Shaddai felt resentment behind those words.

"See that man" -said Shaddai pointing at Juan- "he used to be part of the cartel and he is incredibly weak, I know because I beat them all."

"Hey," Juan replied offended.

"What? No way you beat members of the cartel! Impossible!" said the kid.

"No way you can be part of the cartel, you are weaker than them," said Shaddai teasing them. The gang was offended and started fighting Shaddai with rocks and sticks, Shaddai punched the leader in the face and began beating them all. Juan tried to stop Shaddai, but Carlos halted him.

"He is not hurting them, he is playing with them, believe it or not, Shaddai is good with kids, maybe because he is one," Carlos explained.

"Wow, you are strong, my name is Omid, welcome to Beauty beach," said the kid.

"I am Shaddai, nice to meet you Omid if you train hard maybe you will become strong," Shaddai encouraged him.

"I don't want to be the cartel anymore, I want to be a Shaddai," said one of the kids in the gang. Some of the kids approached Carlos.

*A country of drugs and bullets*

They were amazed by his suit, Carlos showed them his skills, no one was paying attention to Juan. In the distance, a lady noticed the village kids were hanging out at the hill and worried, she ran after them at an incredible speed.

"Stop right there and leave them kids alone..." -said the woman but stopped in the middle of the sentence realizing it was just her old friend Shaddai. "Shaddai, what ya doing here?" said Hannah.

"Hannah!" Shaddai shouted excitedly and hugged her strongly.

"He is a friend of Miss Hannah? She is strong as well," said Omid amazed.

"I came here searching for you! I want you to join my expedition to the old continent,"

"I am glad you are doing okay, after hearing the news, but I can't go with you right now, I am helping this village," said Hannah, a woman with long golden hair, white skin, sapphire eyes, and a great sense of fashion, wearing a light blue blouse and a long deep blue skirt and high heels.

"I see, well, first let me introduce you to my friends, the dude in the suit is Carlos, the weird guy is Juan," Shaddai said.

"Nice to meet you all," Carlos said politely.

"You lied, she is not fat," Juan said.

"Were you saying I'm fat?" Hannah said, hitting Shaddai in the head and leaving him on the ground, she was furious.

"I didn't say you were fat, I said you were soft! Look, let's do it Hannah!" said Shaddai and punched Hannah with all his might in the face, but it was like punching a pillow, Shaddai laughed, and everyone was astonished.

## *A country of drugs and bullets*

"Haven't changed a bit," said Hannah.

"That's why it is fun to hug you," said Shaddai and Hannah blushed.

"Shaddai didn't mention you were a singular," Carlos said.

"Yes, I can enhance the softness and toughness of my body at will but come with me let me show y'all the city, Shaddai, please don't do anything stupid, this place is dangerous," Hanna said and the group followed her.

"And kids, I told y'all not to play far from the city. I can't protect y'all if you aren't close," Hannah Badgered the kids.

"Yes, miss Hannah," said all the kids at the same time.

"So, are you protecting them from the cartel?" Shaddai asked.

"I don't fight them, I hide them and help them run, sometimes I do have to serve as a shield," Hannah explained.

"Why? I bet you could beat them all," Shaddai replied.

"The situation is complex that's why I am asking you to not do anything stupid," Hannah said.

"That's impossible," Carlos added, and everyone nodded including the kids.

"Hey, miss Hannah, let's go to my grandma's. I want her to meet Shaddai," said Omid, Hannah hesitated but agreed after seeing Omid so happy for the first time.

They all arrived at the center of the city, there was a park with a basketball court, all the kids went to their homes, the group followed Omid since he lived near the park, Omid lived in a small house, in a poor town, it was beautiful, but since the cartel arrived, tourism, a big

*A country of drugs and bullets*

part of the economy collapsed. Carlos and Shaddai noticed the state of the houses.

"Hannah, is it okay if we visit them?" Carlos asked worried about being a burden for the poor family,

"Umm, Yeah, I can repay them after, don't worry," said Hannah nervously.

"Grandma, I am here, I brought some friends with me," yelled Omid entering his house.

"Omid, how many times have I told you to tell me before bringing friends" -said an old lady coming to the door noticing Hannah- "Oh my, you didn't mention it was miss Hannah and her friends, come on in," said the lady.

"It's okay, maybe we can come to my place," suggested Hannah.

"No, no, no, do not worry, Miss Hannah, it's a blessing to have you and your friends in my house. My name is Moa, Omid's grandmother, I hope he didn't give you too many problems," said Ms. Moa.

"Yes Hannah, and besides your food is boring and healthy, eww, hello, I am Shaddai, and these are my friends Carlos and Juan."

"I like this man," Ms. Moa laughed, and Hannah glanced at Shaddai.

They entered the house and shared a meal, lentil soup with beans and rice, Carlos was amazed by Ms. Moa's kitchen skills, Juan was grateful since this was his first home-cooked meal in quite a while, Omid was laughing, Shaddai was happy, Hannah was having a good time with her old friend, and suddenly, Ms. Moa shed some tears.

## *A country of drugs and bullets*

"Granny, what's wrong?" asked Omid, concerned.

"There are no tortillas mijo, go for some more," Ms. Moa asked her grandson.

"But we have some more in the fridge," Omid replied confused.

"Those are not good, come on mijo," Ms. Moa said, and Omid left with some coins to buy tortillas.

"It's a true blessing to have you here, I haven't seen Omid this happy in a while, even Miss Hannah looks more cheerful with you around," Moa said with wet eyes.

"No ma'am, your food is the blessing, and well what can I say, I am great, I bet Hannah missed me a lot," Shaddai suggested, and Hannah put up a pouty face.

"Well, you aren't that bad," said Juan.

"Said the modest," Carlos added.

"I sure did, I missed Hannah and we needed a meal like this," Shaddai laughed and Hannah blushed.

"If you don't mind, I would like to tell you what happened to this town, no one that knows comes to visit," Moa said.

"Ms. Moa ya don't have to, these guys can carry themselves," Hannah attempted to stop her.

"No, it's not like that, I just want them to hear me, I haven't expressed my feelings in a long time for Omid's sake.

# Chapter 10

10 years ago, in the state of Crosstruth, Beauty beach was an international destination, a true tropical paradise, with one of the most important ports in the country; life was simple for the citizens of Beauty Beach, some of them dedicated their lives to feed and sell souvenirs to the tourist that visited every year from all around the world.

Abiel, a short brunet man with dark skin and a muscular lean body was the most trusted and beloved man in the town, he was a fisherman and a brave sea warrior. Abiel used to run to Moa's house after every long and successful trip.

"Mrs. Moa, I got you a surprise," said Abiel after knocking on the door.

"Oh, it's you Abiel, how was your trip? Everyone returned safely?" asked Moa.

"Of course, as long as I am here everyone would be safe, anyway, I brought you some lobsters we captured," Abiel answered with a big smile and handed a sack.

## *A country of drugs and bullets*

"Oh my, they're huge! Are you sure you don't want to sell these?" exclaimed Moa after opening the sack.

"Don't worry Mrs. Moa, I have plenty, I hope you gals enjoy them," said excitedly.

"Oh, I see, would you want my daughter to come out, you can talk to her about your latest trip," Moa suggested moving her eyebrows up and down.

"Oh, sure, I mean, I'm all sweaty and, maybe not, it's not like I don't want to see her, but, yeah, sure, maybe another time?" said Abiel laughing nervously with his face all red.

"Sure, you should come for dinner sometime, I can cook these lobsters for you and Astrid."

"Sounds great, but I have to go, enjoy the lobsters, say hi to your daughter from me," said Abiel, walking backwards and leaving.

Every year, Beauty beach celebrated a festival for the town's anniversary. It was popular among tourists, the town square was filled with amusement rides, games, food, and competitions. Like the beauty pageant and the regional fishing contest.

Abiel went to the sea alone in order to prepare for the fishing contest, the winners of the festival had dinner together, Abiel didn't care about the money prize, he had other plans; after sailing for a while he encountered Espada celeste, the biggest and fastest swordfish, in the middle of a storm, they had a duel of guts.

The day of the festival arrived, everyone was having an excellent time, the winner of the couples dance was announced, the winner of the cooking contest was given his price, it was time for the announcement of the queen of the festival, the winner of the beauty pageant, the winner was a young lady with bronze-like skin, black long hair and her eyes were like a dark void, every man was lost on her

*A country of drugs and bullets*

sight, she was the daughter of the former festival queen, Moa, Astrid has been crowned the festival queen and the most beautiful woman in Crosstruth.

At last, it came time for the fishing contest, however, Abiel wasn't listed in the competition, everybody was confused. Nobody has seen him in the last couple of days.

"I thought Abiel was going to show up at the festival for sure, I wonder if he's okay," said Astrid worried.

"I bet he's fine, he's strong," said Moa.

"He didn't see me winning the contest," said Astrid crestfallen.

"Oh, come on, it's not like he doesn't think you are the most beautiful woman around here already," said Moa comforting her daughter.

When the time to announce the winner of the fishing contest arrived, a group of men ran at the town square yelling.

"Stop! Stop! Abiel!" yelled one of the men, and everybody's attention shifted.

"You won't believe what he captured, He is at the seashore," said another man barely breathing due to exhaustion.

"Espada Celeste! He captured the legendary 1,400-kilogram swordfish!" exclaimed the last of the men.

Everybody went to help, and it was unbelievable, the brave warrior of Beauty Beach did it, and although he wasn't listed in the competition, everybody agreed to crown him winner.

The festival resumed, and everybody had dinner at square town, drinking, eating seafood, and dancing until dawn. What a party.

## *A country of drugs and bullets*

"I thought you wouldn't come, I wanted you to see me at the pageant," said Astrid to Abiel, they were sitting alone at the same table.

"In my mind, there was no doubt that you would win," said Abiel.

"I never said I won!" said Astrid, astonished and quite embarrassed.

"You didn't have to, and besides, you're wearing the crown," said Abiel laughing, Astrid was blushing. Abiel took a deep breath and gathered all his courage.

"To be honest, the only reason I caught Espada celeste was so I could sit with the winners at the festival, I knew you were going to win, so I gave everything I got, just to… you know, sit with you," Astrid couldn't stop smiling after hearing Abiel's words.

They dated for a while, the queen of the festival and the king of the seas, that's what the people of the town named them after their wedding, the ceremony was held at the same festival one year later, and one year after that, Omid was born.

However, things changed, a group of criminals came to town, crime started to rise, the cartel wanted Beauty beach for their ports, they asked the sailors for help with the logistics of their illegal business, they refused.

Astrid and Abiel were having a nice walk in the park when one man ran at them.

"Abiel, come with us, some thugs beat up the sailors at the port, you gotta help us," said the man, scared.

Astrid tried to stop her husband but, He just couldn't stay with his arms crossed, so he went to the port.

# Chapter 11

Abiel and his mates ran at the coast as fast as they could, in their way more and more men joined them, people were encouraged to fight for their home, eventually, they arrived at the port, the group of sailors was beaten up, but they managed to resist until Abiel arrived.

"Excuse me gentlemen but there is no place for the cartel in this town," said Abiel daringly.

"We didn't come to negotiate, you are either on our side or you're dead," said one of the thugs shooting bullets, and starting the fight.

The cartel had guns and bullets, the men of Beauty beach were fighting with shovels, pickaxes, kitchen knives, machetes, and guts. Abiel fought bravely with his bare hands and managed to knock a couple of thugs down, but a lot of the citizens of Beauty beach were severely injured soaking in their own blood, but not before fighting back and slashing the criminals with their weapons, after some time, Abiel and his friends won the fight, the cartel had to retrieve scared and injured. They shouted victory and returned to their houses to rest.

## *A country of drugs and bullets*

The tales of Abiel reached every ear of Beauty beach and even on other cities of Crosstruth, "the man that fights for his home", people were inspired by Abiel's doings and started rebelling against the criminals making them step back.

However, Abiel's fame reached the higher ranks of the cartel, and Marti, the regional chief was furious; the port of beauty beach was extremely important for the future of the organization, It was entrusted to him because he was strong, Marti "the chameleon man", He was tall, his skin was tough and green but able to change his colors.

"Chief Marti, the group we sent to Beauty beach was defeated by Abiel and his sailors again," said one of the point leaders in fear, Marti changed his color to red and grabbed him by the neck.

"How the fuck is that possible, he is just a human, I trusted you this mission, I even made you a leader," said Marti pissed asphyxiating his subordinate.

"Well then, I don't have use for the weak in this region," said Marti changing his color back to green and breaking the neck of the point leader letting him dead on the floor, He turned his head to see the other members in the room and notice one thug shaking his legs in fear.

"I don't want cowards either," exclaimed and grabbed the thug by his leg with his long tongue and threw him to the wall and then hit him with his tail in the chest breaking his ribs.

"You guys, bring me a cannonball, let's go to Beauty beach, I'll have to do it myself apparently," ordered Marti and they immediately brought the cannonball to his hand.

Marti and his men went to Beauty beach and arrived at town square, He took the cannonball and threw it at full strength destroying several houses, the thugs started shooting at the houses and pedestrians.

"Come out Abiel! And try to protect your people from me!" yelled Marti laughing.

People started coming out of their houses, and among them, Abiel.

"We'll fight you," said Abiel, staring at Marti and the chameleon glared back.

# Chapter 12

The cartel fought the people of Beauty beach once again, a group of sailors approached Marti, but he finished them with a sweep of his tail and then punched a man into the ground, from the back a man hit Marti on the head with a shovel, Marti turned back and took the shovel from him to hit him back, breaking his skull.

"Everyone, focus on the chameleon man, he is the leader, if we beat him, it's over!" Abiel yelled.

Marti wasn't the only strong person around, Bob the clown, one of the point leaders and Leo the mime another point leader, they were strong as well, they were Marti's right and left hand, Bob used blades as a weapon; Abiel stepped forward beating some lesser thugs in order to fight Marti but was stopped by Bob the clown.

Abiel threw a right straight punch directly to Bob's face, then threw a left body blow and a right hook finishing the combination with

## *A country of drugs and bullets*

a left punch and a right high kick, Bob fell into the ground but bounced back intact.

"My punches are useless, and his body feels strange, he is a singular," thought Abiel.

He kept punching Bob the clown with all his might but without effect.

"Do you seriously think you can beat Marti? Not with that strength!" said Bob laughing before receiving a big punch on the face, Abiel kept fighting, punching, kicking, and dodging Bob's blades, then noticed that Leo was around miming and suddenly Abiel was trapped in a barrier.

Leo the mime was able to create barriers while miming, Bob distracted Abiel so Leo could trap him. With the help of Marti, superior weapons, and with Abiel outside the equation, the people of Beauty beach were defeated, however, Marti kept fighting, men, women even children, it was true horror.

"This will be a lesson for you and the cities around, don't mess with the cartel, don't mess with Marti," said the chameleon man while beating the defeated men and destroying houses of the square town.

Abiel was trying to climb the barriers, but his effort was futile, then, in the middle of the chaos Astrid showed up.

"No," said Abiel, terrified.

"Sweetie, please, run, we can't defeat them," said Astrid to her husband.

"Astrid, get out of here! Now!" Yelled Abiel, and with tears in her eyes Astrid ran, leaving Abiel behind, Marti noticed this and ran after Astrid and grabbed her, taking her down.

*A country of drugs and bullets*

"I remember now, this zone is famous for its women," said Marti to Astrid, looking at her body with malicious intent.

"Leave her alone!" Abiel yelled and started punching the barriers, Leo and Bob laughed.

Marti moved his tongue slowly and licked Astrid's face, she was terrified, and Marti turned his head to see Abiel's reaction. Abiel punched the barrier harder.

"Stop! I'll kill you!" shouted Abiel.

Marti took Astrid from her hair and lifted her then brought her closer to the barrier, Marti laughed and ripped Astrid's clothes in front of everyone.

Abiel started crying and screaming in desperation.

"Don't touch her," said Abiel frustrated, punching the barrier.

"Dear Lord, bless this meal I am about to have," said Marti while looking at the beaten crowd. Abiel was punching the barrier as strong as he possibly could, his fist was covered in blood and his knuckles were cracked, but he kept punching the barrier while crying.

"Please stop," said Astrid's husband, crying.

That day, Astrid was abused over and over, when Marti got bored, he threw her at his men, Abiel closed his eyes, Leo opened a hole in the barrier and Bob stabbed Abiel in the back with one of the blades.

"Who said you could close your eyes," said Bob laughing.

Astrid was abused so many times, she ended up dying, Abiel screamed and cried until he lost his voice, Leo dissolved the barrier because Abiel was weak, Marti approached Abiel.

"Know your place, trash," said Marti to Abiel's weak face.

"Oh, and about your wife," said Marti standing up

"I've had better," Marti added, turning his back to Abiel.

Abiel bled to death, the corpses were hanged in the middle of town square as a message, Abiel's and Astrid's bodies were displayed for 3 days, rotting beneath the sun. Since that day, the cartel was able to use the port without any inconvenience.

# Chapter 13

Mrs. Moa was crying after telling them what happened, Hannah had a tear in her eyes, Juan felt so frustrated since he had experienced the cartel's terror firsthand, his face was red with anger and his eyes were all wet, Carlos was listening with a serious face, but Shaddai, he laughed, he laughed hysterically.

"Wait, Mrs. Moa, is not what you think, Shaddai's singularity," said Hannah trying to explain.

"Don't worry, I know He isn't making fun of what happened," replied Mrs. Moa.

"Hey Shaddai, I don't care if it was because of your singularity, you insensitive prick," said Juan grabbing his friend from his shirt.

"Shut up, and let me go,"- said Shaddai with a mischievous grin that scared Juan, making him fall on his butt- "I wish I was able to meet

*A country of drugs and bullets*

them, they sound fun, Abiel and Astrid," Shaddai added and Mrs. Moa agreed with a weak smile covered in tears.

"Well, that's it, I'll avenge your family, I'm going to fight Marti," declared Shaddai and stood up, Carlos followed him.

"Wait, what are you talking about? I told you to not do anything stupid," shouted Hannah.

"I don't care about this country or about the cartel's business, but how can I stay with my arms crossed after hearing that these people fought with everything they got?, I respect that and besides, the government is not going to help them, if I don't do anything, the blood of these people will be on my hands, so I am going, feel free to join us, Juan you stay with Moa and Omid," Shaddai explained.

"Shaddai, is not that simple, if we go, we'll make everything worse," said Hannah, attempting to stop the group.

They exited the house; Omid was already returning with the tortillas.

"What's going on? Are you guys leaving?" Omid asked.

"Hey buddy, could you tell me where the cartel lives?" Shaddai asked, looking at Omid directly in his eyes with a smile.

"Is down the main street, in the middle of the jungle at the right of the coast, but why? What's happening?" answered Omid worried after seeing Hannah's concerned face.

"I'll be back in a moment," Shaddai promised, patting Omid's head.

Shaddai stretched and ran at top speed, Carlos followed and Hanna ran as well.

## *A country of drugs and bullets*

"Wait, Shaddai, stop, let's talk about it," Hannah yelled.

"I am with you on this one, something has to be done, but, do you have a plan?" Carlos asked.

"Yes, we need a plan, we can't just run into their base," Hannah suggested.

"Sure, we can, I am getting excited, I really need to punch these people," Shaddai shouted.

They crossed the jungle in the blink of an eye and found a big mansion in the middle, it was built with marble and gold, it was covered with a big and expensive wall of steel.

"Here we go!" -Said Shaddai kicking the door of the wall knocking it down- "WHERE IS MARTI?"

The snipers on the roof shot the group, the bullets didn't have an effect on Carlos and Hannah covered Shaddai, all bullets bounced back from her body.

"Sadness," -exclaimed Shaddai raising his hands and making all the snipers and guards fall crying- ``I don't need you to protect me, Hannah," Shaddai added.

"Ungrateful prick," Hannah replied.

From the interior of the mansion a Chameleon man got out with 2 women wearing bikinis on their knees walking like dogs, they were on a leash, Hannah saw that and recognized them, She got angry.

"Those ladies went missing recently, I am glad I followed you, Shaddai there is no going back."

*A country of drugs and bullets*

"What's going on? Why is everyone crying on the floor?" said Marti pulling one of the ladies from the leash, hurting her. Bob the clown and Leo the Mime were behind Marti.

"Oh look, it is the beautiful Hannah, can I keep her?" asked Bob the clown.

"Nah, I called dibs on her," Marti replied and Shaddai laughed.

"I am going to enjoy beating you so much, Marti," said Shaddai daringly.

"Oh! So you might be one of those heroes that are always attempting to free these people," Marti replied, looking down on Shaddai.

"No, heroes kick butts, I came for your head," Shaddai replied and Marti laughed at him.

"Very well then, let's fight, let's step into the jungle, I don't want to destroy my house."

"Ok," said Shaddai following Marti to the jungle.

"Shaddai, it's a trap," Carlos warned, concerned, Hannah tried to stop Shaddai, but Bob got in her way challenging her.

"I know, but I won't lose," answered Shaddai, making Marti chuckle. Carlos ran after them, but Leo created a barrier getting in Carlos' way. Shaddai and Marti jumped the wall and ran until they got lost in the jungle. The fight began.

*A country of drugs and bullets*

# Chapter 14

Shaddai and Marti walked between the trees, they suddenly stopped in the middle of the jungle.

"I see, you wanted to fight here so you can camouflage, right chameleon man?" Shaddai asked.

"Well, it depends, maybe it won't be necessary," Marti replied.

Marti turned and threw a punch, Shaddai answered with a straight punch, both fists collided leaving an impact due to their strengths, Marti swept his tail, Shaddai jumped dodging and kicking Marti's jaw, Shaddai followed his combination with a jab to the solar plexus and a right hook to the body, Marti punched Shaddai in the face

*A country of drugs and bullets*

with his right hand and then hit him with his tail on the body, Shaddai grabbed the tail and pulled to uppercut his opponent, Marti flinched.

"You might be small, but you have good punches, who taught you how to fight?"

"My uncle," Shaddai answered.

"You know I wanted to be a professional boxer," Marti added.

"Aww the poor baby couldn't achieve his dreams because society rejected him, that's why he became a criminal, you see no one cares about your backstory, nobody cares about trash like you, so I am done with the small talk," said Shaddai touching a nerve and continuing the fight.

Shaddai approached his opponent and connected an uppercut to the solar plexus, followed by a kick in the liver, Marti spat blood, Shaddai grabbed his foe's head and hit him with his knee on the nose, then a straight punch to the chest, sending the chameleon flying through a tree.

Marti shot his tongue and grabbed Shaddai from his left ankle, Shaddai was disgusted and then pulled by the reptile's tongue, Marti hit him to the ground, Marti then jumped and tried to stomp Shaddai's skull but he rolled dodging the attack.

Shaddai stood up, both of them planted their feet and exchanged blows for several minutes, Marti had the advantage in reach and size, but Shaddai was faster and stronger. Marti stepped back and stretched.

"Ok, time to stop playing, you are pissing me off," said Marti, changing its colors, He was invisible now. Shaddai was surprised and was suddenly hit in the jaw, then in the body, and after that hit behind the knees, he was knocked down.

*A country of drugs and bullets*

Shaddai rolled and stood as fast as he could but was punched several times in the face. Shaddai lifted his guard to cover the punches, but they came from all directions. Shaddai was sent flying through a tree scarring the birds.

The young man stood up again just to be pummeled, but Shaddai couldn't stop smiling he started laughing, Shaddai laughed louder after every punch, He began to bleed, and his laughter changed to an ominous tone.

"Happy mode, hyperactive body," said Shaddai, glowing a yellow tone.

# Chapter 15

While Shaddai was fighting Marti, Hannah and Carlos struggled with Leo and Bob, Hannah was in a hurry to help Shaddai, so she wanted to finish her fight as fast as possible, She punched Bob in the face making him bounce back, she kicked her opponent in the ribcage and the proceed to thrash the clown but she was unable to inflict damage. Bob tried to stab Hannah, but the blade broke since Hannah's body was hardened.

"I have to be careful; I don't want to mess up your cute face, ha, ha, ha," said the clown.

*A country of drugs and bullets*

"Don't worry, I'm not that fragile," Hannah replied.

Meanwhile, Carlos was trapped inside a barrier jail made by Leo the mime, Carlos attempted to break free punching, kicking, tackling, and shooting mental bullets and balls to the wall, but he wasn't able to crack the barrier, he was cornered, however, Leo wasn't able to damage Carlos either since his suit was protecting him. The fights weren't moving forward, and they wanted to go with Shaddai.

Hannah ran and kicked Bob in the face, guts, and then again in the chin, she slapped him grabbing his head and smashing it to the wall breaking it.

"You hit like a girl, he, he, he," said the clown mocking Hannah, then she punched him again leaving another hole in the wall.

"I see, your body should be made of rubber or some sort of plastic, that's why y'all are immune to my kicks," said Hannah.

"Maybe, maybe not, ha, ha, ha, maybe you don't have to know, we only have to stall you until Marti is back, he, he, he," said the clown making Hannah angrier, she looked at the women on the leash and started thrashing Bob again.

"Hannah! Calm down! Don't waste your energy!" said Carlos trying to remain calm and to think of a solution.

"What should I do then?" said Hannah, angry.

"Let's change opponents, if you can break this barrier I'll deal with Bob," said Carlos.

"Like we'll let you do whatever you want, hi, hi, hi," said Bob, but Hannah punched him in the face, shutting him up, then she grabbed the clown from his ankles to spin it and threw him towards the mansion breaking the windows.

## *A country of drugs and bullets*

Leo stood there confident in the toughness of his barriers, Hannah then kicked it with her heels smashing the wall into small pieces, the mime was astonished.

"Thanks," said Carlos and ran after the clown.

Leo tried to stop him, but Hannah intercepted him and punched him with her right fist in the jaw, a left punch to the body, she toughened up her nails and slashed Leo leaving a deep cut, the mime was bleeding, Hannah finished him with one high kick to the chin, breaking Leo's teeth.

Carlos approached Bob, throwing a jab, a straight punch, and a kick to create some distance between him and his foe, then he proceeded to charge an attack with his hands, he started creating a big green sphere of aura.

"Mental Blast!" Carlos exclaimed and shot the aura sphere, Bob confident, received the attack and went straight to his head, but this time was effective, the mental energy messed with the clown from the inside leaving him convulsing on the floor.

"You deserve it" - said Carlos looking down on the clown. - "I'll need a stronger aura output or another way to use my mental energy."

Carlos left his opponent and went where Hannah was.

"Y'all are finished up there?" Hannah asked and Carlos nodded while walking to her.

"Ok, let's go with Shaddai then."

## Chapter 16

Marti hit Shaddai nonstop, right hook, jab, uppercut, tail sweep, low kick, knee to the guts, but Shaddai was laughing, after a while, Shaddai spat blood to Marti's face.

"Now I can see you," said Shaddai before punching the chameleon really fast.

Marti was still hard to see even with the stains of blood, he managed to land some hits on Shaddai, but every hit he landed was responded with 5 from Shaddai. The difference in speed was vast,

*A country of drugs and bullets*

Marti shot his tongue attempting to wrap Shaddai and restrain him, however, Marti couldn't camouflage his tongue or any other organ that wasn't his skin, Shaddai grabbed Marti's tongue and pulled it, ripping it off.

The chameleon bled from his mouth and returned to his regular color because of the pain, Shaddai ran after him punching him.

"Happy bullets!" - Shaddai casted a rain of jabs on Marti's torso sending him back to a huge tree- "That was for Abiel."

Marti tried to get on his feet, but Shaddai kept pursuing him.

"Happy shotgun!" -Shaddai hit his opponent with a straight punch to the jaw pushing him through the tree taking it down- "That was for Astrid."

Marti tried to stop Shaddai, he was scared but without his tongue, no words came out of his mouth. Shaddai lifted him from the floor with a kick.

"Happy tomahawk!" -Shaddai exclaimed connecting a hook to the liver, Marti coughed blood- that was for Moa, and this is for Omid, Happy bazooka!" shouted Shaddai punching Marti's ribcage with both fists sending him some meters back leaving a mark on the ground.

"Ha, ha, ha, ha! I actually felt how your ribs broke with that one, it felt great, I want more, I'll make you feel the agony of these people with my own fists," said Shaddai, smiling ominously.

Marti cried, he crawled and ran screaming, his desperation was heard by everyone in Beauty beach, Shaddai hunted him down.

"These are for everyone at Beauty beach! Happy Gatling gun!" Shaddai yelled, thrashing Marti with a full range of combos with all of His might and speed behind every punch. Jab, uppercut, jab, straight punch, hook, punch to the guts, left uppercut to the chin, punch to the ribs, blow to the liver, the combination was so fast that Shaddai's fists went invisible.

Dust rose from the ground, the land was shaken, trees fell left and right, the animals of the jungle ran from the scene, even at a distance, you could see the havoc of the battle. Marti's bones were broken, piercing through his organs, his skin was covered in blood and bruises, his body was getting swollen.

"Yes, yes! That's more like it, I can feel your muscles being ripped by my knuckles."

Marti screamed and cried louder, Shaddai finished with a strong right punch that sent Marti flying; however, Shaddai grabbed him by the tail to stop him, but the strength was so big that he ended up ripping Marti's tail.

Shaddai threw the tail to the side, it was still moving, Marti's body however was beaten to a pulp, left without breath. Shaddai was covered by the blood of his enemy, he took a few steps, got closer, and spat on Marti's body.

"Know your place trash."

# Chapter 17

Hannah and Carlos walked through the jungle, they followed the fallen trees and the trail of the battle, eventually, they found Shaddai, Marti's body lying on the ground Shaddai was standing next to it covered in blood.

"Is he" -Hannah was astonished by the scene- "is he dead?"

"Yeah, I think so," Shaddai answered, smiling at Hannah.

*A country of drugs and bullets*

"Why? How? Shaddai," Hannah was having trouble processing the scene.

"What do you mean why? You know what he did, he deserved to die."

"But it is not your job to decide whether he lives or not," Hannah replied, concerned.

"Who decides then?" Shaddai asked.

"The authorities, God, that wasn't ok," Hannah tried to explain.

"The government is on their side, and are you telling me that in the eyes of God he didn't deserve to die? And if I sin, am I the one who deserves punishment?" Shaddai asked Hannah.

"I won't judge you, but I am a little concerned, don't you think that this was the result of bottling your emotions? And after knowing what happened around here you exploded, that could be dangerous," Carlos expressed, hinting that He didn't agree with Hannah's approach to the situation.

"I'm a psychologist as well, y'all don't have to talk to me like a child y'all don't need to be subtle, right now I'm worried as a friend," Hannah replied annoyed by Carlos' words.

"Maybe you don't know Shaddai that well then," Carlos said.

"Y'all don't understand the situation, Shaddai is still not showing how he truly feels," Hannah replied.

"Hannah, I don't need you to judge me or talk to me about how what I did was wrong, and Carlos You don't know how my singularity works, both of you ignore how I feel, we don't perceive emotions in the same way, I know what I did," Shaddai said.

"You did it for them, right? You knew that if you showed up with Marti defeated, the people of Beauty beach would kill him. You didn't want them to carry that in their conscience, am I right?" Hannah questioned.

"Does it matter? Even if we left Marti alive the police would free him after he recovered, causing problems to more people," Shaddai said, Hannah was disappointed and crestfallen but at the same time, she was relieved.

"But it's important that you know that it isn't your responsibility, you don't have to carry the guilt and decisions of others. But It's done, so what now?" Carlos asked, Shaddai lifted Marti's body.

"I'll take responsibility, I'll give the body to the people of Beauty beach, once everyone knows that Marti is dead, the police won't have a choice but to do something about the rest of Marti's men."

The group returned to the mansion, they tied up Marti's men and carried them back to Beauty beach town square, on their way, Shaddai started telling people to come with them, so everyone knew. The town square got full really quick.

Omid and Moa arrived happy knowing that Shaddai and his friends were safe, Juan was relieved as well, Shaddai got on top of Marti's men stepping on their backs.

"Listen, everybody, Marti is dead! His men are incapacitated, I killed him, I am sorry for what happened, I am sorry You had to go through everything, but I have a gift for all of You, that's what I need everyone to gather around," Shaddai explained, some people were confused, others couldn't believe it, some, like Moa cried and thanked because it was over, Shaddai waited until the crowd was bigger.

## *A country of drugs and bullets*

"You will deliver these men and the body to the authorities and tell them it was me, but for now is time to celebrate. You don't have to deal with the cartel anymore, so here is your gift," Shaddai yelled so everyone could hear him.

Shaddai raised his hands and extended them towards the multitude and said, "Happiness! Happy Hour!"

After Shaddai's words, everybody started laughing, Juan, Moa, Omid, all the people that were hurt, traumatized, and abused by the cartel, was able to laugh again, Hannah felt better after seeing this, Carlos was calm, some sailors took Marti's body and his men to jail, everyone was processed and they informed the authorities about what happened, the party started.

People started gathering what they had and without the worry of the Cartel Tax they started buying stuff for the party, they started cooking and putting up speakers, people were dancing, drinking, and celebrating. Mrs. Moa cooked some Lobsters for Shaddai.

"Look, this was Abdiel and Astrid's favorite meal," said Moa, offering buttery lobsters, however, Shaddai hated seafood but didn't want to be disrespectful, so he gave it a shot, surprisingly, Shaddai liked lobsters, he also tried crabs, although he still hated fish and shrimps, He was having a good time eating Moa's dishes.

Hannah went to the families of the freed women, those who were under Marti's chains. She hugged them and cried for not doing something about it before, for ignoring the situation, and apologizing for her naivety.

Carlos and Juan drank with the sailors telling each other good stories, everyone was having a great time.

*A country of drugs and bullets*

Chapter 18

The authorities of Beauty beach reported the incident to the government of Crosstruth, they decided to transfer the thugs to a federal prison, the report only mentioned Shaddai as responsible since that was the agreement to avoid problems for Hannah which was in the country with a permit and Carlos since he is a citizen of Moon's navel;

## *A country of drugs and bullets*

Shaddai crossed from Eagle nest without a permit, so it was going to be harder to track.

A group of sailors helped transfer the thugs to the federal prison, Carlos helped in case Leo or Bob attempted to escape. Hannah went to a different city to treat the freed women, Shaddai and Juan stayed with Moa and Omid.

Moon's navel government was furious after receiving the news of Marti's death, the relationship between them and the cartel was delicate, to say the least, however, Marti's dead was already public knowledge; they attempted to take credit for it in order to calm the people of the country that were tired of the corruption and insecurity, but the news of an unregistered young man named Shaddai fighting the cartel spread around Moon's navel like wildfire.

Newspapers, news broadcasts, and independent reporters, all of them were talking about the chaotic wave of events in the country. The caravan of immigrants crossed the border and keep moving forward, the crimes kept rising, a group of civilian rebels started fighting the cartel, Shaddai, the man that executed the regional chief of Beauty beach is slowly becoming a symbol of revolution, rumors of a terrorist organization lurking around the country, the 8 swords army could be inside Moon's navel.

Meanwhile in Tower city.

"Phee!"

"Shaddai is on the T.V. Why is he fighting the cartel? I hope Carlos doesn't get involved in this," said Tisha worried.

Meanwhile in Riverstone in the panda chocolate store.

"Ha, ha, ha, Honey, you are crazy, I hope I see you again because after this, some big sharks will go after you," said Cupcake laughing nervously.

## *A country of drugs and bullets*

The news traveled even to the most remote places in the country, including the cartel's main hideout, Chopo's house. A secret mansion made entirely of gold, with its own jungle full of tigers and rivers, Chopo, the head of the cartel, was having a meeting with all the state bosses.

"Red hair and green eyes, a few months ago the government gave us a job to erase a family living in this country, in exchange, they gave us freedom in some important operations, since this guy is unregistered, there is a possibility that he escaped us and is now searching for revenge, he might not be alone, however, we don't know if he is working with the government or if the government gave us that task in order to gain an enemy so we can destroy each other," said Chopo to his men sitting in a golden chair with two blue tigers at his sides.

"If you allow me to add something, Don Chopo, I know Shaddai, the reason he is unregistered is that he's from Eagle Nest," said Chuck from Tower city, state boss of Snake crawl.

"Go on," said Chopo, allowing Chuck to speak.

"I met him while I was on a trip in Eagle nest, I doubt he is searching for revenge, more likely he had a disagreement with Marti, everybody here knows that guy was a creep, I know about his singularity and since he attacked one of my operations, I would like to ask you if I can take care of him instead."

"Eagle nest huh? If we kill him, Eagle nest will be all over our business, good, take care of this situation," Chopo ordered.

"Don Chopo, but what about me? I am the one who should take care of Shaddai. The bastard destroyed my most important operation," suggested the Crosstruth state boss.

"No, let Chuck take care of this, You need to go to the federal prison and get rid of your men, we don't want any of our secrets to be

## *A country of drugs and bullets*

public domain"- Chopo said and everyone agreed.- "Now we have other issues to discuss, bigger problems," Chopo added.

Meanwhile in the great pine, the presidential house of Moon's navel.

"The 8 swords army, we shouldn't have taken that job from the universal church, even if we passed the task to the cartel, the consequences are now bringing chaos to my government," said Henrick Pine, president of Moon's navel.

"Do not worry my leash, the army is on their way to deal with this situation to ensure our truce with the cartel remains intact!" said Rodrigo Perez, the general of Moon's navel army.

Meanwhile, in a hidden tunnel in Angel town, capital of Angel Den, a red-haired man with a black short beard, black clothes, and a sword on his waist grabbed a newspaper with Shaddai's smiley face on the cover.

"Shaddai, you idiot, you had to come to this country, anyway, you being here might be helpful," said the red-haired man while walking through the tunnel arriving at the core of the cave where his men were working.

"Quetzalcoatl, take the other 2 and pay Shaddai a visit, things might get ugly from now on, this incident actually saved us some time," said the man to a giant feathered serpent.

"I'll do, admiral 5," answered Quetzalcoatl in a deep voice.

"After you take Shaddai, come back to the den and wait for my orders, I'll proceed with the mission to move forward with the plan," said Admiral 5.

*A country of drugs and bullets*

# Chapter 19

Juan and Shaddai were playing basketball at the town square with Omid and some kids, waiting for Carlos and Hannah to come back, suddenly it started getting windy, a helicopter was approaching the town square.

## *A country of drugs and bullets*

"Omid, everyone, go back to your houses and don't go out," said Shaddai to the kids.

Everyone ran following Shaddai's orders, however, Juan stayed, the helicopter landed, Chuck, Orange, and Koko got out of the helicopter, Shaddai was surprised.

"Long time no see, Shaddai, how ya doin kiddo?" greeted Chuck kindly.

"Chuck! How are you, buddy? You look strong!" said Shaddai, happy to see his friend. Juan was left speechless and terrified at the fact that Shaddai was friends with the state boss of Snake Crawl.

"Do ya remember this guy?" asked Chuck

"Yeah, I think they visited you once at the hospital, chimpanzee and yellow right?" Shaddai answered.

"First of all I am a Gorilla man, not a chimpanzee, and second my name is Koko," said the Gorilla upset.

"And my name is Orange, not Yellow, how could you miss that? Just look at my clothes," said the tall man wearing orange clothes. Shaddai laughed.

Juan was sweating nervously, but his friend was chatting casually with some drug lords.

"Anyway, what are you doing here Chuck?" Shaddai asked.

"We saw ya in the news, you should've mentioned that ya were coming to Moon's navel, you did a lot of damage to the cartel's structure in your last adventure," Chuck answered.

"I am sorry, my trip here was unplanned, and it wasn't my intention to fight the cartel, they just got in my way and sometimes it was just self-defense."

"That's what I thought, but you still did a lot of damage, and the cartel can't unsee this mess, you dismantle a point in tower city, one of the most important locations due to its multiple roads to the border cities and the main access to Eagle nest, and this port is really important to ship to the south of the new continent and the east coast of Eagle nest," explained Chuck.

"Wait, you know a lot about the cartel, what's up with that?" Shaddai questioned.

"You don't know who these are?" asked Juan.

"Hey, you are the missing guy, Juan, it seems like you betrayed us," said Orange.

"I see, we'll deal with that later, ya know the rules, but more importantly, Shaddai, I joined the cartel, I am one of the top dogs, the very head of the cartel sent me here for ya, but since ya are my friend and I know ya, I want ya to join us, with your strength and singularity it'll be a great help, you can maybe replace Marti."

"What? How and why did you join the cartel? After what happened to you," Shaddai replied.

"I realized something Shaddai, powerful people can do whatever they want, there are no good nor bad, just powerful and weak people, what happened to me was the result of me being weak, but thanks to the cartel I am not weak anymore."

"I am sorry but that is going to be a hard pass for me buddy, I have no intentions on working for the cartel," said Shaddai.

## *A country of drugs and bullets*

"I knew it wasn't going to be easy but is either bringing ya as an ally or bringing your corpse, however, we don't want Eagle nest's officers in our business, so why make this an international problem Shaddai, so please consider, in the meantime, I'll show ya the benefits of being in the cartel, I'll be waiting for you at Marti's mansion," Chuck replied, Chuck and Koko, closed their eyes.

"Orange flash!" yelled Orange emitting a bright orange light, leaving Juan and Shaddai blind for a few moments.

Orange kicked Shaddai in the back sending him towards Koko, the gorilla man threw an uppercut at Shaddai sending him to the sky, Orange hit Shaddai once again with an energy ball, Chuck jumped and then punched Shaddai sending him back to the ground and destroying a part of the town square with the impact leaving a huge hole on the ground, Shaddai was left unconscious.

Moments passed, in his sleep he felt sorrow, anger, and fear from the outside, this awakened Shaddai from his slumber, he was in Hanna's arms, she was crying really loud, then he noticed Carlos, he was angry and scared, a lot of people were around the area, confused he stood up trying to process what happened.

"Shaddai, what happened?" said Carlos.

"Well, a couple of friends came to visit me, it turned out that my friends joined the cartel and they invited me to be part but after I refused, they attack me and" -said Shaddai before noticing Juan's corpse, Chuck and his friends murdered him and hang the body in one of the basketball nets, the habitants of Beauty beach took down the body and it was now laying on the ground. -"Juan?" Shaddai asked while shivers ran through his body after seeing his friend's cold body covered in blood.

Shaddai turned his back and understood why Hannah was crying and why Carlos was worried and mad, he clenched his fists, tightened his jaw, the pressure of his feet shattered the cement under him, Shaddai was furious.

"Hannah, Carlos, follow me, we are going to Marti's mansion," said Shaddai.

"Wait, we need to," Hannah said but Shaddai stopped her.

"It wasn't a question."

Shaddai dashed into the jungle, Carlos and Hannah followed him.

## Chapter 20

Shaddai, Carlos, and Hannah ran through the jungle towards the mansion again.

"I know Chuck, they caught me off guard. He wasn't a singular when I met him but he is strong now," Shaddai said.

"What do y'all mean he wasn't a singular?" Hannah asked.

"That's not important for now, the important thing is that we have information about their powers, Chuck is accompanied by 2 guys, 1 is a Morpher, a gorilla-like man, the other is an Elementalist he can emit light and energy from his body, knowing that they want me on their side I bet they'll try to tire me before I met Chuck, so we might encounter them around here, however since the news only mentioned me, they ignore your existence, that's our leverage, you guys deal with Orange and Koko I'll deal with Chuck."

Carlos and Hannah were astonished, they've never seen Shaddai so serious about something, they agreed and continued until they were ambushed by Orange, the group was blinded by a fluorescent flash. Orange shot a barrage of energy blasts directed to Shaddai but Carlos made a barrier of green aura with his mental energy.

"I knew you weren't alone, doesn't matter as long as we can drag you to chuck," said Orange, throwing more energy blasts.

"It seems like I am the perfect opponent for this guy, we have similar singularities and my suit prevents him from blinding me, I'll protect you until you recover your sight, then continue without me," said Carlos to his friends.

"Orange blast."

"Mental blast," Carlos and Orange threw energy at each other, colliding and making an explosion. Shaddai kept running and Hannah followed.

"I'll leave it to you dude," said Shaddai, trusting the fight to Carlos.

"Aren't you going to try to stop them?" Carlos asked Orange.

"Nah, as long as Shaddai is alone at the mansion, Chuck will take care of business," Orange replied and with his hands, he conjured a sword made of orange energy, He slashed but Carlos stopped it with a mental shield.

Hannah and Shaddai advanced but they were intercepted by Koko. He was swinging at the top of the trees, he jumped towards Shaddai throwing a punch, but Shaddai countered it and sent him flying, Shaddai then ran after him and kicked him in the face.

"Hannah, I don't want to waste time, you can easily deal with this one," yelled Shaddai and moved forward.

"Wait, it'll be faster if we fight them all together, don't go alone Shaddai," Hannah replied.

"If you want to come with me, finish him fast," said Shaddai running.

"It's now you and me, cutie pie," said the Gorilla and punched Hannah in the face, She softened her body absorbing the damage, Koko kept punching Hannah with amazing strength but it was like beating a sponge.

"What the hell?" said Koko, confused.

Shaddai kept running, and eventually, he arrived at the mansion, his old friend Chuck was waiting inside.

# Chapter 21

Koko dashed towards Hannah, He punched her several times with all his might, Hannah fell on the ground and took the punches, Koko's punches shattered and shook the ground, but Hannah absorbed the damage.

After a while Koko stopped and stepped back, Hannah stood up and dusted herself up, Hannah tried to attack Koko but he dodged every attack, he was quite agile and the jungle gave him an advantage since he was really good at moving through the trees.

"I'm unable to hurt her, and I don't want to waste energy, if this keeps going on I'll run out of stamina and lose, maybe punches won't hurt her but I can grab her soft body and twist her up, I bet I can rip one of her hands," Koko thought while climbing the trees dodging Hannah.

"I won't be able to catch him, right now he thinks I am only able to soften my body so, Him ignoring that I can harden is my best shot to win fast, I need him to come and get me," Hannah thought and started running towards the mansion.

"Damn it, who said you could leave, we are fighting!" yelled the Gorilla man pursuing Hannah.

Koko threw a punch, Hannah dodged, and kept running, Koko surpassed her and tried to tackle her, Hannah dodged again.

"Why is she dodging? Is she aware of my plan? I need to throw some punches, she'll try to absorb the damage, and then I'll grab her."

Koko launched some jabs, Hannah dodged, Koko threw a big right hook, Hannah softened her body and absorbed the punch, left punch, and then Koko threw a straight punch with all his weight behind it.

"This is my chance!" Hannah thought hardening her body like a diamond, Koko punched Hannah in the face but broke his fists, Koko bent over the pain.

"Nail pistol," Hannah said, hardening one of her fingers and leaving a hole in Koko's chest.

Koko grabbed her arm and twisted as hard as he could, but Hannah hardened her body again rendering Koko's plan useless.

"Why? Why is your body so hard?!" Koko yelled frustrated.

"Diamond kick," said Hannah, throwing a hardened kick on Koko's skull leaving a crack.

"Nail gun!" Hannah hardened her hand and nailed his fingers on Koko's body leaving five more holes.

Koko laid on the ground, Hannah tried to run, but Koko grabbed her by the foot and threw her away breaking some trees, he stood up and dashed towards Hannah one more time, took a deep breath, and proceeded to attack, Hannah hardened her body and ran after Koko, both of them exchange several blows, Koko punched her on the face, on the ribs on the chin, Hannah punched him on the guts, on the liver, and on the nose, after a while, Koko kneeled losing the exchange but lifted his guard covering his head with his arms.

Hannah slashed Koko's arms leaving some deep cuts, when his guard went down, Hannah punched Koko to the ground with a hardened fist.

Hannah sighed and stepped on one of Koko's knees breaking it, Koko yelled before getting unconscious

"Now you can't follow me," said Hannah and started running towards the mansion.

## Chapter 22

Orange launched a bunch of energy blasts, Carlos dodged and ran into the woods hiding behind the trees waiting for an opening, after a while, Carlos charged towards his foe shooting mental bullets, Orange dodged.

"Orange Blast."

"Mental Blast," Carlos and Orange said at the same time shooting big energy balls from their palms, they collided leaving an explosion.

Carlos ran and hid again in the woods, but Orange found him time and time again.

"It seems like his aura output is larger than mine, no, it should be similar but since part of my mind is charging the suit he has the advantage, I'll run out of energy first, but thanks to my suit I am more resistant and probably stronger in physical combat, so I need to get close even though close combat is not my specialty." Carlos thought while dodging Orange's blasts.

Carlos dashed forward, Orange attacked but Carlos didn't stop, deflecting the blasts with a small mental shield, they got closer, Carlos threw several hits, but Orange dodged, Carlos kicked Orange in the guts then hit him with a solid straight blow in the chin sending him flying.

"Mental Blast!" Carlos yelled, launching a green energy ball hoping to finish his opponent, but Orange stood up and with his hands created an orange light sword.

Orange cut in half Carlos' mental blasts, He slashed through it and kept swinging the light sword aiming at his opponent, Orange Bashed but Carlos deflected the attack with a mental shield, Orange slugged but Carlos ducked and answered with a right punched infused

*A country of drugs and bullets*

with mental energy straight to Orange face, Orange withstood it and ravaged Carlos with one big swipe, sending him to the ground and a few meters away.

Carlos stood up and stopped charging his suit for a second,

Orange dashed towards him attempting to finish it.

"Focus, aura output" -Carlos's thought, after charging mental energy he turned on his suit again and created a green light sword. - "Mental blade." Orange and Carlos clashed; their blades collided several times for a few minutes.

"You are pretty good with the sword for a beginner," said Orange.

"I'm no beginner, I used to spar a lot with Shaddai, he is really good as well," Carlos replied.

Their swords collided once again but this time Orange disappeared his sword, Carlos lost balance as a result and Orange blasted him in the helmet, Carlos punched him in the face breaking Orange's nose.

Orange bled and replied with an orange beam that impacted Carlos' breastplate, sending him across the jungle through several trees. Carlos struggled to stand on his feet but he got up one more time.

"Orange Barrage!" Orange yelled, sending a lot of energy balls towards Carlos but he replied with the same amount of mental blasts leaving a big explosion. Orange casted his light sword once again.

"Mental blade," Carlos said after taking a deep breath and casted his mental green sword. Orange prodded but Carlos parried, their swords clashed.

## *A country of drugs and bullets*

Carlos yelled, focusing more energy into his blade making it bigger, shattering Orange's blade, Carlos ravaged his opponent, slashing his opponent's chest.

"Psycho Cut," Carlos said while the blood of his foe splashed on his suit. Carlos hit Orange in the head and then stomped it.

"Mental blast!" Carlos shot a big mental aura ball finishing his enemy.

"Thank you for teaching me a new technique," said Carlos, tired, he walked a few steps.

"I need to improve my close-range attacks," said Carlos, removing his helmet and sitting under a tree and taking a break, he was exhausted and with no energy left.

# Chapter 23

3 years ago, in Tower city, Chuck was having dinner in a fancy restaurant with her girlfriend Isabelle. They were celebrating their anniversary in their senior year of high school.

"So how was your trip to Eagle nest?" asked Chuck

"Great, I needed to go shopping, so it was fun, hopefully, I can go again soon," answered Isabelle, she was a brunette woman with brown skin from a rich family.

"Maybe we can go this summer, weather will be nice, we can even go to Friendland's beach," replied Chuck, he was dressed in a black suit and a confident smile, he also came from a powerful family in tower city.

"I'd rather go to the malls, beaches in eagle nest aren't that good don't you think?" said Isabelle.

"It depends, but in general I agree, however there are some amazing places to be in nature, maybe we can rent a cabin in Hogsfield," Chuck suggested.

"Sounds fun," said Isabelle before taking a sip of her glass of wine.

They had dinner, a peaceful chat in general, a charming evening, they eventually left the restaurant, Chuck was driving a black S.U.V. They arrived at Isabelle's house, they parked and sat down on the sidewalk holding hands and watching the stars.

A couple of white trucks suddenly parked around Chuck's vehicle, and a group of armed thugs got out of the trucks, aiming at the couple.

"Give me the keys of the car man," yelled one of the thugs.

*A country of drugs and bullets*

Chuck covered his girlfriend, Isabelle was scared, Chuck was nervous.

"Ok, I'll give you the keys," Chuck said, cautiously.

"Hands up," said another of the thugs putting a gun to Chuck's back. They raised their hands slowly, while the thugs searched for valuable items in their pockets, one of them found the keys in Chuck's pocket, Isabelle started crying.

"Why are you doing this?" Isabelle mumbled.

"Shut up," yelled one of the thugs hitting Isabelle in the face with the gun.

Chuck tried to defend her but he was shot in the guts, and the thug behind him shot him at the back of his neck leaving Chuck bleeding on the sidewalk; the thugs left in their trucks, and one of them took Chuck's SUV.

Isabelle called for help, Chuck was treated in a hospital in tower city, once he was stable, his family sent him to a huge hospital in Eagle nest. Chuck was in a delicate condition, unable to feel his legs, unable to move any of his limbs, but he was receiving the best treatment possible, at least he had regained consciousness.

"Yo!, do you have a minute to discuss the word of the living God?" said a young Shaddai, who was visiting the hospital preaching words of hope to the ill.

"I do have time, but I don't believe in god and even if he exists, I'm pretty sure he hates me."

"It feels like that some days huh? But maybe we aren't that special to have a God picking on us for a hobby," said Shaddai laughing.

*A country of drugs and bullets*

"I'm sorry, I do believe that God likes us, but we are just unable to comprehend, I'm just here because a friend makes me do this, well I do owe a lot to the people in that church, and I need to be here to make people feel better, so maybe is destiny that you and I met here."

"Well, if that's the case, destiny sucks."

Months passed, Chuck and Shaddai started to get along, Shaddai started visiting Chuck more often, they became friends and Chuck was recovering faster.

"I see. So that's what happened to you, I have family in Tower city, so I hope they are doing alright, it sounds dangerous, I should visit them one of these days, maybe I can visit you as well, once you recover," said Shaddai.

2 young males enter Chuck's room, Koko and Orange, Chuck's high school best friends, came from Moon's navel to visit him. Chuck introduced Shaddai and they all got along just fine. On their final day visiting him, they told Chuck that Isabelle continued with her life, that She needed to move on, date other people, but that she wishes Chuck the best.

His friends left, his girlfriend abandoned him, unable to walk and or feel anything, Chuck didn't have any strength to do therapy, He just wanted everything to end.

"You know, I can help you feel better you know?" said Shaddai.

"I know, you are trying to help," said Chuck, hopeless.

"No, what I meant back there is that I can make people feel better, I am a singular just like your friends, I can control the feelings, emotions of some people, I can give it a shot for you," Shaddai replied.

"What? You could make me happy all this time? Why did you never mention it?" Chuck yelled frustrated.

## *A country of drugs and bullets*

"Well for starters it might not work, second of all if I make you feel happy that won't change anything, you'll just laugh, but you won't process what happened to you in a healthy way, sadness is powerful you know?" explained Shaddai. Chuck remained silent, disappointed.

"Ok, I'll give it a shot, so please cooperate," said Shaddai, Chuck swallowing saliva nervously.

"Happiness," exclaimed Shaddai pointing at his friend. Chuck started giggling slowly then he started laughing, after a while it got louder, Chuck was laughing hysterically with tears on his eyes and snots on his nose.

"I NEED TO BE STRONGER SHADDAI, ALL THIS HAPPENED BECAUSE I AM WEAK," yelled Chuck laughing crazily.

Chuck started to give everything he got to therapy, starting to feel, starting to move. Shaddai was there to help him occasionally, but Chuck was so obsessed with recovering physically that he ignored the fact that he needed to recover emotionally, the therapy ended and Chuck and Shaddai parted ways.

"See you, buddy, take care and I hope I can see you again someday," Shaddai said.

"I wouldn't be able to do it without you Shaddai, thanks for everything," they said goodbye with a big smile on their faces.

Chuck went back to tower city. He fully recovered there and started training, running in the morning, going to the gym, lifting weights in the afternoon, and learning mixed martial arts at night. Chuck wanted to bring the thugs to justice, so he went to the police department to see how the investigation was going, but to his surprise, there was no advance, not a clue, not a hint, nothing. Not only did Chuck recognize one of the cops, but he was also one of the thugs that shot him that night, he gave up on the investigation at that moment.

*A country of drugs and bullets*

He started attending church, the church of the living God, the church of the existing god, the enlightened temple, and even the universal church. Chuck wanted answers but had no patience, he soon resented God, society, and everyone around him, that's when he started training with more intensity.

2 years passed from the incident, Chuck was driving around tower city at night in his new car around a bad neighborhood, he was stopped by a car with 2 thugs on it, they pulled it from his car wanted to steal it, but Chuck stroke one of the thugs with one devastating blow, pull out a crowbar and hit the second thug in the head. He beat them to a pulp and tightened them up and took them in his car.

Chuck drove outside tower city, to the desert to torture the thugs, searching the location of their immediate boss, eventually, Chuck got the location of their point. Chuck took the thugs to that place where he met Miss Aurora, the point leader.

"You have some nerve, beating my men and starting a fight with the Cartel, and You, you guys should feel ashamed, being defeated and giving information, you are useless," said the woman moving her whip ready to punish them.

"First of all, I didn't start anything, as a matter of fact, I came here to replace them, I want in and I wanted to prove my worth by beating them and torture the information out of them," Chuck replied.

"You should be dead right now," Aurora added.

"I have nothing to live for, so if that's the case I don't care, but at least I am better than these pieces of crap," Chuck said.

"It doesn't make sense, why he wants to get involved in the cartel voluntarily, and I don't think he is a spy since we are allied with the government, and even if he was, this strategy is to direct, I'll test him," Aurora thought.

## *A country of drugs and bullets*

"Here, take this gun and kill these useless bastards" -Aurora ordered Chuck- "If he is a spy, he'll hesitate and I don't think he will" - But Aurora's thoughts were interrupted by the sounds of the gun, Chuck shot the men killing them without blinking.

Chuck was accepted as a thug, he was efficient and ruthless, since he was an upper class he was able to sell a lot of his product, soon he was recognized and started his own point, as a point leader he recruited Koko and Orange his best friends and since they were singulars Chuck's point quickly became one of the strongest and most profitable, his operations grew until he became a regional chief, however, he was still weak, he had money, power but he wasn't able to compete in combat with a singular.

One day he was summoned to a highly secret meeting with some state bosses, a priest, a governor, and the head of the cartel, Chopo. The cartel was able to finish a mission trusted to them by the Moon's navel government and the church, in return the cartel was prized with an experimental serum, it has been perfected through thousands of years, back then the rate of success was a mere 1%, the universal church spent centuries researching that serum in secret, now the rate of success is 70% the people who received the serum and fail, die, the people that succeeded were granted a mutation resulting in an artificial singularity.

He was chosen to be a recipient for the new formula of the serum, in his quest for power he accepted knowing the risk, the injected a red dark liquid in his body, his muscles swelled, he yelled in pain, he felt like he was being burned from the inside out, his veins popped out and after a few minutes of agony, he woke up with inhuman strength.

Chuck saw one of the thugs that shot him that night when he was with Isabelle and punched him in the head killing him.

"Sorry boss, it was a reflex," said Chuck smiling, the priest, the governor, and Chopo were really pleased by the results, and started a negotiation. Chuck's region grew stronger and in one year after joining, he became the state boss of Snake Crawl.

# Chapter 24

Shaddai entered the mansion and walked into a big hall. Chuck was sitting at the other side of it in a big white chair, waiting for Shaddai.

"Ha, Ha, ha, you look angry Shaddai, sorry for the mess I left, but I had to do it, nothing personal, I also wanted to show you how strong I've become thanks to the cartel," said Chuck excitedly approaching Shaddai.

"I understand the truth of this world, powerful people can do whatever the fuck they want. Since I like you, I want you to be at my side, but I also wanted to show you that I am serious, you come with us or you die, to teach you that life is not a game," Chuck added but Shaddai kept walking.

"That's where you are wrong, I am not playing" -said Shaddai and started screaming, he clenched his fists, his veins popped out, he screamed louder and his fangs grew, Shaddai's muscles swelled, he suddenly went from an average body to a strong muscular build, Chuck flinched and Shaddai screamed louder, his skin slowly turned a glowy red- "Angry mode, furious body," said Shaddai in a deep voice.

Chuck quickly approached Shaddai throwing a punch, Shaddai did the same, both fists collided but Chuck's knuckles broke due to the impact, jab, straight punch and a body blow from Shaddai threw Chuck to the floor.

"You little piece of," Chuck yelled but was interrupted by a barrage of hits from Shaddai ending in a big shot to the guts, Chuck spat blood and stepped back slowly. Chuck threw a wide left hook,

*A country of drugs and bullets*

Shaddai dodged, Chuck cover himself with his arms and Shaddai proceeded to ravage his guard breaking Chuck's upper arms.

Chuck dropped his guard and Shaddai planted a fist on his foe's face, throwing him to the end of the hall. Chuck promptly stood back up fearing for his life, Shaddai pummeled his enemy and sent him to the ground leaving a hole in the mansion's floor, Shaddai grabbed Chuck's left leg strongly, breaking his opponent's tibia, and threw him against the ceiling bouncing back to the floor leaving some cracks.

"Wait Shaddai, please don't do this, if we team up, maybe we can..." Chuck said with regretful tears.

"As I said I am not playing, Juan told me about the universal church meetings with the cartel, artificial singularities huh? Do you know what was the cost for your new powers? What was the price the cartel had to pay? Hundreds if not thousands of lives, the security of people like you, who were just hanging out with their girlfriends, the security of people like the ones living in this town who are kind and hard-working," yelled Shaddai while Chuck was scared.

"The lives of people like my family!" Shaddai added, punching Chuck in the face.

Chuck crawled, Shaddai walked slowly to finish him, Chuck stood up again very weak with blood all over his clothes.

"I didn't know about your family, I had nothing to do with it, I'll help you, please Shaddai, don't do this, aren't we friends?" Chuck begged.

"You were right about one thing, strong people can do whatever they want, but there is always someone that can beat you, and you are still weak" - Shaddai threw a big and wide left hook at Chuck's chin, ripping his jaw apart and tossing it to the other side of the room- "Angry tomahawk."

*A country of drugs and bullets*

Blood splashed all over the place, Chuck's body was on the ground, but Shaddai wasn't satisfied.

"Wait!" -said Hannah running to Shaddai grabbing him from the back in an attempt to stop him, Shaddai grabbed Hannah from the head and tossed her to the floor- "You are not like this Shaddai," said Hannah with a broken heart.

Shaddai recognized Hannah's face and reverted to his normal state, he remained silent crestfallen, Hannah hugged him and after a few moments, he hugged her back.

## Chapter 25

Chuck and his friends were defeated, but it wasn't time to celebrate, the people of Crosstruth gathered at Juan's funeral. He was remembered as a kind person, gentle with the kids of Beauty beach, a person who understood the struggles of the Crosstruth's folk. Even though most of his existence was torture, he never stopped hoping for a change, his death was a reminder of all the innocent people who died in the cartel wars, but also a reminder that things are starting to look better, everyone was there at the funeral, everyone except for Shaddai, he was nowhere to be found, he knew that if he was seen at the memorial people would ask him to use his singularity to laugh once again, but Shaddai knew that it wasn't time for parties and dances, sometimes it is time to sorrow, to cry and learn, he wasn't going to belittle the death of his friend, also, Shaddai was full of guilt in his heart.

Carlos gave a speech, at the funeral, Hannah was with Moa and Omid comforting them, the people of Beauty beach couldn't stop wondering if they bring a curse upon everyone who stood for them, but at the same time, they were fighting to hold into hope, thanking the efforts of Shaddai, Carlos, and Hannah.

Meanwhile, in every other place of Moon's navel, chaos, big news all around the country, 2 state bosses and 7 regional chiefs from the cartel have been defeated, Chuck the drug lord from Tower city and responsible for the criminal activities in Snake Crawl was defeated by the same man who overthrew Marti in Crosstruth, Shaddai who was no longer an unidentified person, it was now public information that he was from Eagle nest and was working together with Hannah another singular from Eagle nest and Carlos a singular from Snake Crawl both of them responsible from the fall of a regional manager, Koko and Orange respectively. The other state boss and 4 of the regional chiefs

*A country of drugs and bullets*

were defeated by a group of civilians and singulars that formed a rebellion. On another note, more rumors of the 8 swords army were being spread.

Tisha and Phee were surprised to see Carlos on the news, grateful to see that he is doing alright but angry at Shaddai for involving Carlos in such dangerous matters.

The people of Moon's navel had mixed feelings about Shaddai, even though he was fighting the cartel, he was causing a lot of conflicts around the country or at least that's what the media said about him, the idea of him and Hannah being from Eagle nest started some conspiracy theories, people started to believe that the Eagle nest was causing the rebellion to provoke a civil war and take advantage of a weakened country, others thought that the Eagle nest was sincerely trying to help and because of that they sent Shaddai and Hannah, others believed that it was everything orchestrated by the 8 swords army, and the rest didn't have a clue, but everyone knew something for a fact, a giant storm of events was about to hit Moon's navel.

The 8 swords began to move according to their agenda, Henrick Pine executed a military order, the government of Eagle nest received the news and found out Hannah's and Shaddai's location, from the southern and northern borders, and even from the center of the country, the capital, the navel, the ones with power started to move.

## Chapter 26

A couple of days passed and Shaddai was having trouble deciding whether or not to leave Beauty beach. He wanted to protect its citizens in case the cartel wanted to retaliate, but at the same time as long as Shaddai was there, people were in danger.

He tried to discuss it with Hannah and Carlos, but suddenly Beauty beach was surrounded by tanks, large vehicles full of soldiers, one of the tanks shot straight into a neighborhood, destroying a bunch of houses.

"Carlos, go and gather as many people as you can and put them in one of your mental barriers, Hannah and I will fight them," Shaddai suggested nervously.

"What the hell are you talking about, I can help more if I fight with you," Carlos replied, another tank shot making an explosion, Carlos gave it up and followed Shaddai's advice.

"I'll take care of the tanks, y'all beat as many soldiers as y'all can," Hannah said while hardening her body.

"Roger that, happy mode, hyperactive body," said Shaddai glowing yellow.

"If I end up as a terrorist and unable to do missionary work, I won't forgive you Shaddai," Hannah added.

"Pretty sure that should be the last of our concerns," said Shaddai and ran after a full squad.

A tank shot Hannah, after the smoke disappeared, she was standing with some of her clothes ripped, she blocked the shot with her arms.

*A country of drugs and bullets*

"I am definitely not in a good mood," said Hannah, frowning. She ran after the tank with her hardened body deflecting bullets and kicked the tank's turret destroying it, she stopped one of the vehicles and punched the truck's chest leaving a hole in the engine, grabbed it, and threw it to a soldier.

"Happy Gatling gun!" yelled Shaddai punching through the Moon's navel infantry. One of the soldiers shot a Gatling gun at Shaddai but he dodged the bullets, jumped, and kicked him in the jaw.

"Merry bullet," said excitedly, punching another soldier.

"Happy shotgun," shouted Shaddai, punching a man in the chest and leaving him unconscious.

A soldier shot a bazooka at Shaddai, but he grabbed the missile and threw it back at a tank. Meanwhile, a group of soldiers with Gatling guns found Carlos, but he was able to block the bullets with his mental shields. He created a small dome to protect the residents of Beauty beach.

"Happiness! Now tell me why you are here," said Shaddai, making some of the fallen soldiers who were still conscious laugh.

"To erase this town!" said one of the soldiers laughing.

"We need to bring your heads to the cartel to prove we are still on the same side," said a lady with an intense evil grin. Shaddai stopped his happy mode.

"We'll kill you and everyone here and then say that you died fighting crime bravely," said a soldier, laying on the ground.

"That's it, I am done with this place! Furious body!" said Shaddai, transforming, kicking, and punching the soldiers, breaking legs, arms, and rib cages.

## *A country of drugs and bullets*

More and more soldiers gather around Carlos trying to break the mental dome.

"I'll have to let go, and fight with them, so please run and find a safe place, I'll just waste my energy here," Carlos said

"No way, this is our home, we are going to fight for it," said one of the fishermen of Beauty beach.

"Yes, you've done enough, it's our turn!" said a lady who was inside the metal dome.

"Please don't act irrationally, I am unable to stop you but please consider this, if you are afraid grab the children and flee if you want to fight, follow me!" said Carlos using the mental dome to create a big green, fluorescent flash that blinded the soldiers and freed the villagers. Carlos immediately shot mental bullets at the soldiers leaving them out of battle and charged with some sailors, fishermen, and villagers following him.

Shaddai punched some tanks dismantling them, helicopters and more vehicles and soldiers arrived, a squad started shooting him in the back, a soldier shot a bazooka and hit Shaddai's chest, a tank shot hitting Shaddai's head sending him through a wall of one of the houses.

Hannah was getting hit with Gatling guns, a helicopter flew over Hannah and shot her with the turret. Carlos arrived with a mental blade and cut the helicopter's weaponry and slid one of the vehicles carrying men.

"Confusion," said Carlos with a green glow on his eyes paralyzing the squad. Hannah proceeded to pummel those men. Another helicopter flew towards them, but Shaddai grabbed a rock and threw it at the helicopter's propellers, taking it down.

*A country of drugs and bullets*

"I have a secret weapon, but I might get unconscious after this attack, so you must finish the fight after it in case more reinforcements arrive," communicated Shaddai.

Carlos and Hannah agreed.

"Sadness, sad," Shaddai said but it was interrupted when a fast water stream fell from the sky cutting a tank.

"Was that your secret weapon?" Carlos asked.

"Of course, no, I am not an Elementalist like my brothers," said Shaddai, annoyed, a big roar was heard from the sky, and from the clouds, a big feathered serpent appeared. A woman with black clothing and dark blue hair dropped from there with a sword made of water, she was able to cut through the tanks and vehicles manipulating the water. A coyote man also wearing black with 2 machetes in his hands also jumped from the feathered serpent, slashing through the infantry. The flying feather serpent took down every helicopter.

"Who are they?" Carlos asked.

"Don't worry," said the blue-haired woman.

"We are here to help," said the Coyote man.

"We are allies," said the Quetzalcoatl landing.

"Seems like there is no choice but to fight together," Hannah suggested.

"Very well then, I'll save my new attack for when it is perfected, but now I'll do this," said Shaddai gathering the Beauty beach folk that were fighting.

"Madness!" yelled Shaddai lifting his hands towards the villagers, making them angry and giving them a little push in strength.

## *A country of drugs and bullets*

The sailors yelled and ran to the battle, Quetzalcoatl and his friends fought alongside Shaddai, Carlos, Hannah leading the Beauty beach people against the moon's navel army. Until they eventually retrieved.

Everyone was exhausted, Quetzalcoatl and his friends approached Shaddai.

"Sorry for not introducing ourselves properly, I am Quetzalcoatl, the coyote man is Nezahualcoyotl, the blue-haired girl is Tlaloc, we are members of the 8 sword's army, we work under the leadership of admiral 5, who directly ask me and my friends to come for you."

"Nice to meet you, I have no idea what you are talking about, but thanks," Shaddai replied.

"They are a big organization of terrorists, or at least that's what the United Nations decided to tell us," Carlos added.

"This one is smart," Tlaloc added.

"I know who they are but why would they want me?" Shaddai asked.

"You are kidding me, right?" Hannah added.

"Allow me to explain, you've become a symbol for the rebellion, we are currently helping the rebels in their efforts to overthrow the government, even though we have a different agenda we can benefit from this, but in order to win we need to fight coordinately we can't do that without you guys, not just Shaddai but Hannah and Carlos as well," Quetzalcoatl explained.

"Very well then, that explains a lot, but I don't think I should leave this place yet, not after knowing the country is after my friends,' Shaddai replied.

*A country of drugs and bullets*

"Don't take this the wrong way, but the reason they want to destroy this place is that you are here, they won't stop until they get you, you hurt the relationship of this country's government with the cartel, but they are willing to kill civilians just to get you," explained Tlaloc.

"Yeah, we are your best shot of leaving this country alive, unless the Eagle nest army gets involved," Nezahualcoyotl said, and his stomach grumbled.

"What if we all discuss this with dinner," said Mrs. Moa who was hiding with the children of Beauty beach.

They all have a humble nice dinner, between the destruction the battle left. Shaddai and Carlos decided to leave, Hannah was struggling to make a decision.

"Sweet mother of God, this food is amazing," said Nezahualcoyotl, eating as fast as Shaddai.

"Thanks for everything Shaddai," said Omid trying not to cry.

"You are welcomed," Shaddai replied smiling.

"Do you think I can be like you?" Omid asked, Shaddai remained silent for a moment.

"What if instead of trying to be like me, you focused on being a better you? I mean being an Omid is pretty neat too, don't you think? Said Shaddai laughing after thinking for a while.

"I am going to miss you guys, playing with you... and Carlos, and miss Hannah ... and Juan, but I won't cry, I'll be strong, I'll smile proudly," said Omid with a cracked voice.

"There is nothing wrong with crying once in a while," said Shaddai, and Omid Cried loudly, Moa and most of the people of

## *A country of drugs and bullets*

Beauty beach cried as well. Hannah decided to go along with Shaddai after talking with Tlaloc for a while. They finished the food and said goodbye to everyone.

"Very well then Quetzi, take us to our next destination," said Shaddai sitting on Quetzalcoatl.

"Please don't call me that," said Quetzi. Hannah, Tlaloc, Carlos, and Nezahualcoyotl also sat on Quetzi, and the feathered serpent flew, taking them away until they were covered by clouds.

# Chapter 27

Quetzalcoatl flew through the skies, Shaddai was sitting at the front having the time of his life, Carlos was feeling a little dizzy and Hannah didn't like wavy movement and she was terrified.

"You'll get used to it," said Nezahualcoyotl.

"Yeah, and besides even if you fall you can harden your body," said Shaddai laughing at Hannah.

"If I fall, I'll drag y'all with me," said Hannah with her eyes closed and grabbing onto Quetzi firmly.

"You know? It isn't necessary to hold that strongly is kind of hurting me," said Quetzi complaining

"I am sorry but, I ain't stopping it," replied Hannah.

"By the way, Quetzi, where are we going exactly?" asked Shaddai.

"To our secret base, we are going to be there for a while to hide all of you, also we are waiting for orders from our admiral," replied Quetzi, a little annoyed by the nickname.

"I see, and where exactly is that secret base?" questioned Shaddai.

"It's Angel Den around angel town," answered Quetzi

"Wow you really revealed the location of your super-secret base," said Shaddai laughing.

### *A country of drugs and bullets*

"Well we are thousands of meters in the sky and no one can hear us, besides, at this point, there is no way you are working for the government," replied Tlaloc.

"And it's not like people could easily find the base with that information," said Nezahualcoyotl.

"Why is that Nezi?" said Shaddai.

"What did you just call me?" asked Nezi but the conversation was interrupted, Quetzi started to land, increasing the speed, Hannah Yelled, Carlos by inertia tried to grab something, holding Tlaloc.

Quetzalcoatl saw a volcano and approached it.

"Wait, we aren't landing there, right? Asked Hannah.

Quetzalcoatl flew into the volcano, it went dark and a few dozens of meters down a bunch of holes, the group entered one of them and followed the tunnel.

"This region is known for its volcanoes, so we created some fake ones and made a tunnel system, so even if they found out the fake volcanoes, they'll just get lost in the tunnels, but nobody cares about a few extra small volcanoes since there are a lot of them in Angel den," Quetzi explained and kept flying until he found the base.

The base was a big hole with more tunnels and different rooms illuminated by some shining cyan mushrooms, the base was covered by a light blue tint and people were wearing black clothes, it was like their uniform. Quetzi landed, and the group got down, Hannah was relieved to be on the ground.

"Mr. Quetzalcoatl, welcome back," said a warrant officer with a small group of men.

## *A country of drugs and bullets*

"Nice to be back with you guys, the mission was a success, we stopped the Moon's navel army, and Shaddai, Carlos, and Hannah are on our side," said Quetzalcoatl and one of the men there was writing every one of his words.

"Send my report to Admiral Shane and now that we are on the subject, any words about him?" asked Quetzalcoatl, Shaddai reacted to that name.

"Yes, sir, Admiral 5 contacted us, he is already in the location and is waiting to execute his mission," said the warrant officer.

"You guys follow me, I'll give you a tour around the base," said Tlaloc, taking the group while Quetzalcoatl finishes the protocols of the reports.

The base was filled with everything needed to live there, a kitchen with ground ovens and some appliances, and professional utensils, dorm rooms, they were small and shared between a large group of soldiers to save space, and a big area to train, with lift weights, a boxing ring and weapons all of them surrounded by a track field.

"Great, I'll be able to train here," said Shaddai excitedly.

"I see, you want to get stronger for the fight, that's the spirit," congratulated Tlaloc.

"Is not just that, I realized that my furious body state is still unstable, and I am still developing my new technique," said Shaddai.

"How are you planning on training your singularity?" asked Hannah.

"By getting in shape, if my body is stronger, my singularity will be stronger as well, so it's time to get sweaty."

*A country of drugs and bullets*

"Speaking of sweat, you are full of sweat, blood, and dust. It is time to change your clothes and take a shower," Nezahualcoyotl added. Hannah was excited and all of them went to a room full of clothes.

"How? Why? So many clothes" expressed Hannah, amazed.

"When we need to go outside, we go undercover as civilians, also we have bases in 8 countries, all of them overseen by one admiral, so we have clothes from all around the world, we have everything you need here," Tlaloc said to Hannah.

She picked a dark pair of pants, a deep blue shirt, and a king blue blazer matched with a pair of high heels of the same color and a pair of sapphire earrings, she took a long shower and fixed herself. Hannah was happy and radiant.

Carlos grabbed a pair of jeans and a long sleeve shirt with light and dark green stripes. Shaddai took a dive into the clothes and picked some sandals and dark gray shorts, but he suddenly stopped and got serious.

"Are you okay dude? Asked Carlos.

"Need help with the outfit? Like seriously, I can help you," added Hannah.

"I can't believe it," said Shaddai crestfallen.

After a few silent moments, he grabbed a black t-shirt.

"Everyone look, this shirt has a small hedgehog on it, is perfect and so cute," said Shaddai happily with tears in his eyes.

"Shaddai is so dumb," thought Hannah and Tlaloc.

"Behold, Hannah this is true fashion," yelled Shaddai putting the hedgehog T-shirt on.

## Chapter 28

A few weeks passed, Shaddai ran on the track field every day for hours, lifting gigantic weights, after all these days he was able to lift one ton in base form, he started to have a more defined lean body. Working out shirtless and sweaty, Hannah noticed.

"Why are you hanging out like that, all nude? Put on a shirt," yelled Hannah.

"And get my awesome hedgehog shirt all sweaty, I'll pass, thank you very much," said Shaddai, who wears his hedgehog shirt every day after working out and taking a shower, putting it on the laundry once a couple of days.

"And besides, it's not like I am bothering anyone, soldiers here often work out shirtless, it's hot down here you know" - added Shaddai taking a few steps and getting closer to Hannah. - "It isn't like I am provoking inappropriate thoughts into someone, right?"

Hannah blushed and her face turned red like a tomato.

"I mean not you, right? You are pure like a nun," said Shaddai smiling, but this offended Hannah.

Carlos was at the other side, he stopped using his suit, reading every day, and meditating to improve his mental aura output and energy manipulation skills. But after these weeks he put the suit on again and walked towards Shaddai.

"99 wins, 100 loses, it is my time to choose the challenge, and I am going for a good old-fashioned fight," said Carlos daringly.

## *A country of drugs and bullets*

"Feeling confident huh? Well, I want to test the results of my training as well, let's give it a go," said Shaddai accepting the duel and both of them stepped into the ring, Hannah and Tlaloc were particularly interested in the fight.

They started the fight, both of them dashed to the center of the ring and exchanged hits, straights, uppercuts, counters.

"You've improved your close combat skills," said Shaddai, hitting Carlos.

"I only lost that time because I wasn't used to the suit," replied Carlos, returning the favor with one body blow.

"Excuses, very well, I won't hold back, happy mode, hyperactive body!" exclaimed Shaddai and disappeared, Carlos made a mental shield to protect himself, but Shaddai broke through it with a punch hitting Carlos in the helmet, jab, straight punch, jab, uppercut, jab, right hook, left, hook, jab, one-two, Shaddai gave a barrage of hits to his foe.

Carlos tried to counter but Shaddai dodged.

"He is way too fast," said Tlaloc, kind of worried.

"Shaddai is way stronger now," Hannah thought.

Carlos casted a mental blade and swung it against Shaddai trying to hit him but he dodged everything.

"As I said, no holding back, angry mode, furious body," said Shaddai, transforming.

Carlos made 3 barriers, but Shaddai shattered all of them and hit Carlos on the chest making him flinch back to the ropes. Shaddai went to finish the fight.

"Shaddai wait!" exclaimed Hannah.

Carlos started glowing green and summoned a solid armor around him with four extra arms and said, "Mental armor, Ashura mode."

Tlaloc's jaw dropped.

Shaddai hit Carlos with everything he got, Carlos covered himself lifting his guard and using two of the extra arms, Shaddai threw a barrage of frenzy hooks, Carlos' suit, mental armor, and even an extra pair of hands on his guard and it wasn't enough to protect Carlos, the mental armor was starting to crack. But Carlos used one of the free mental arms he had and punched Shaddai on the face with a full-strength counter. Shaddai fell unconscious.

"100 wins to 100 wins now," said Carlos and emerged victoriously. Tlaloc's eyes sparkled a little.

After a few minutes, Shaddai woke up.

"You are incredibly strong with your angry mode, any longer and You could've actually killed me after breaking my mental armor, but you are not as fast and you don't think as clearly, technique is one of your strengths, but in this form, you fight differently, with more openings to counters," said Carlos giving feedback to Shaddai.

"You maybe could've won with just your hyperactive body, maybe you should stick to that strategy until you fully mastered your anger, and thanks for showing me that my mental armor is still weak, I wanted to improve my close combat skills in case I am forced to fight that way, but I should think in one more strategy, just in case,"

"Thanks, dude, glad I could help," added Shaddai with a big smile on his face and a mild headache.

## Chapter 29

Chopo's Mansion and main hideout of the cartel in the middle of a dense jungle of Moon's navel, it was guarded by snipers on top of a golden wall that surrounded the mansion, the insides were protector by hitmen, one of them was walking on the gold streets of the gigantic property but suddenly blood started to rain, the snipers were dead.

The hitmen gathered in a formation to protect each other's back, but it didn't matter one hitman fell on a puddle of blood, one of his companions checked the corpse and it had a deep cut on the throat, then another hitman fell facing the same destiny, and another, one by one, all of Chopo's guards were dying.

All of them died bleeding slowly while their breaths were taken by a quick but deep slash, in the middle of the bodies walking down the main street towards the main building, Chopo's house, a man with a black jacket, red hair, a dark beard and a sword stained with blood, Admiral 5, Shane.

Shane entered the mansion and killed the members of the cartel who were inside, they weren't able to say a word, the admiral entered Chopo's chamber it was a long hallway with waterfalls on the sidewalls and marvelous sculptures of gods, at the bottom a big diamond chair and 2 purple tigers.

"Red hair, brown skin, and blue eyes, so it was true," said Chopo and the tigers stood up getting ready to attack but they were scared.

"Let your tigers free, I don't want to kill them," said Shane.

"I see, go on, let the man fight, when I am done with him, you can eat him," said Chopo and the tigers ran away.

"I am admiral 5 of the 8 sword's army and I came for your head."

"Oh I know all about you, the government suspected the presence of the 8 sword's army so we worked together to eradicate all the suspects, turned out to be your family, but the government didn't had into consideration the side of the family leaving in eagle nest, we were searching for redheads and most of your family living in eagle nest has white hair, well, is not like Moon's navel wanted Eagle nest as an enemy," explained Chopo.

"The moment you worked together with the universal church you had your days counted, this fight is way bigger than a simple cartel, or a corrupt country and now both will fall," Shane added.

"Well, I don't have anything against you in particular, but now that you killed my men, I will finish the job, I can't imagine how grateful the church is going to be with me after I give them your corpse, and you will be with your family again," replied Chopo and created a sword of gold with his bare hands."

"An Elementalist who can create gold," said Shane, unsheathing his sword.

"The perfect singularity to build an empire," said Chopo walking towards Shane.

"It's a pretty stupid ability, the power to devalue a metal," said Shane.

Both of them dashed and clashed their swords creating an impact that caused a wave of air through the mansion. Chopo slashed,

## *A country of drugs and bullets*

Shane blocked, the head of the cartel pierced but the admiral parried. The sound of the blades colliding filled the hallway, Chopo created a wave of gold to crush Shane, but he pierced the floor with his sword and hundreds of blades grew from the ground colliding with Chopo's gold.

The shockwave created after the collision of the attacks destroyed the mansion they were fighting in, the swords clashed hundreds of times, Chopo grazed Shane's jacket with his fingers and it started to turn into gold, Shane took off the jacket and stepped back, the slashed again and their blades collided.

Chopo launched cannonballs of gold from his palms, Shane cut through all of them, and after minutes of exchanging combinations of attacks, Chopo managed to touch Shane's right arm and it was turning to gold, Shane stepped back and cut his arm with his sword before he was turned into a statue.

"Bwahahaha, next time will be your legs," said Chopo, the most wanted man in the world.

Shane started to bleed a lot, it was like a crimson river, more and more blood came out of Shane's wound, and he moved his arm splashing some blood in Chopo's face.

"Well, this is not the first time I have your blood all over me, Bwahahahaha," said Chopo and started to get itchy, he dropped the sword and screamed.

"Burns! It burns!" yelled Chopo.

Shane dashed and with one big sweep cut Chopo's head and stepped on it.

"You underestimated the power of my blood," said Shane and screamed, growing his right arm back. He sheathed his sword, grabbed

*A country of drugs and bullets*

Chopo's head from his hair, and took a communicator from his pants' pocket.

"Tell Quetzalcoatl I finished the mission, move on with the raid on Navel," said Shane through the communicator, walking towards the jungle and tossing the head to the tigers.

# Chapter 30

Everyone gathered in one spot inside the secret base, Quetzalcoatl, Tlaloc, and Nezahualcoyotl were waiting for everyone to discuss the admiral's instructions.

"Everyone, Admiral 5 has defeated the head of the cartel, is our time to move and proceed with the next mission, so, in order to proceed, we are going to separate in smaller groups and go to the capital, to the Navel using different routes, once there we are going to reunite and meet the rebellion, the fight will take place in the celebration of independence day, outside Willow house, the presidential residence, you will receive your next orders once we meet with the rebellion," explained Quetzi.

All the soldiers started leaving with their groups on different days, Shaddai, Carlos, and Hannah traveled to the Navel with Quetzi, Nezi, and Tlaloc. A few days passed and everyone arrived at the Navel, the biggest city in the country and the most populated on the whole continent, that fact allowed people from the rebellion and from the 8 sword's army to hide in plain sight, some had to wait outside the city due to their high profile, like Quetzi and Shaddai.

Captains and sergeants of the 8 sword's army met with the leaders of the rebellion, to avoid grabbing attention this important meeting was attended by a handful of important people, like Quetzi's trio and their assistants, Shaddai and his friends, and some familiar faces from the rebellion's side, Phee, Carlos' brother who joined the rebellion after hearing about his brother misadventures, Cupcake, who left her store to help Shaddai.

"Hannah," said Cupcake

"Cupcake," said Hannah, there was a weird tension between them, some sort of secret rivalry.

"Hey, what are you doing here?" asked Carlos to his brother.

"Phee!"

"Wait, you guys joined the rebellion as well?" Shaddai asked the other members who appeared to be Shaddai's friends.

Zamudio, a white tall guy with brown hair, his singularity allowed him to create explosions, Mike, a green-eyed man with dark curly hair his singularity allowed him to manipulate sound, Jorge a short man with dark hair, his singularity allowed him to create magnetic fields.

"Well, we aren't going to allow that you do everything here," said Mike

"Having a weak person like you as the symbol was bad, so we had to join," added Jorge.

"Pretty sure I can take you," Shaddai replied.

"Who told you to act like the main character?" asked Zamudio.

"No one, that's the difference between you and me, you wait until something happens to join the action," said Shaddai provoking Zamudio.

*A country of drugs and bullets*

"Enough, we have things to discuss," yelled Tlaloc.

"We need to work together in order to take down this government, they have 4 pillars, the president, Henrick Pine, The general of Moon's navel army Rodrigo Perez, Mouette Pine the first lady, and a bridge between the government and the biggest media company of this country, and last, the head of the cartel, Chopo," Added Nezi.

"Our Admiral already took care of him, he killed him, but because of that he won't join us in this fight," said Tlaloc, and everyone was shocked after hearing what happened to Chopo.

"I see, so we will have to take care of the remaining 3 pillars," Jorge added.

"Phee,"

"This is the plan, in the middle of the president's speech, the rebellion will present themselves as regular citizens, the army already suspect an attack, so they will surround you, that's where we enter, we will divide our forces in 2 to support you from the left and from the right, Nezahualcoyotl will lead the left forces and Tlaloc the right one," Quetzi explained.

"Actually, I have an idea, I've been working on a new technique, I can take care of one of the sides, so the rebellion can focus on defending from one side, and the 8 sword's army can direct all its might to the other side to corner Moon's navel forces," Shaddai interrupted.

"Of course, you have a new technique," Mike critiqued.

"Oh, Honey, that will be dangerous," said Cupcake.

"He can take care of himself," said Hannah daringly, and Cupcake glared at her in response.

*A country of drugs and bullets*

"How reliable is this technique?" Quetzi questioned.

"Worst case scenario, I take care of a big chunk of the army, but I will need to be dropped at the center of the army and I will need someone to cover me since I don't know how tired I'll get after this technique," Shaddai answered.

"I can cover y'all," Hannah suggested.

"Didn't you say he can take care of himself?" Cupcake mumbled/

"It needs to be someone that can resist my singularity," Shaddai added.

"I can go, but honestly, I think I might be more useful defending the rebellion using my mental shields," Carlos added.

"Very well then, Hannah can back you and I will drop you both, the rebellion will face the remaining forces of Moon's navel from the front, Nezahualcoyotl will support you attacking them from the back, Tlaloc, you and your men will wait to see how Shaddai and Hannah are doing, in case they fail you attack from that side, in case they succeed, support Nezahualcoyotl," Quetzi decided.

Shaddai clenched his fists excitedly, Phee took a good look at Carlos' suit to upgrade it and fix it.

"Since I can fly, after dropping Shaddai and Hannah I will face the president in Willow house, you guys try to locate the other 2 pillars in the middle of the fight," Quetzi finished explaining the plan.

*A country of drugs and bullets*

## Chapter 31

Henrick pine was at the balcony of the presidential residence, the willow house, people from all around Moon's navel traveled as every year to celebrate Independence Day and yell at midnight the names of their heroes, but this time was different, this time wasn't about independence it was about revolution, people were tired of the corruption of their government. The surroundings were tense, soldiers, trucks, and helicopters were swarming around the capital, civilians locked themselves in their homes knowing it was going to be a violent night.

"Dear citizens of Moon's Navel today we reunite once again to celebrate the independence of our nation, I find myself with joy for being here with such an amazing crowd, welcome to the national palace, we welcomed our governors, our generals, and all the soldiers who are here in order to protect us, giving their lives for this country,"

The rebellion heard the president's speech disgusted, but they were aware of their surroundings, the army was getting closer

### *A country of drugs and bullets*

surrounding them, they were prepared to sacrifice the lives of every civilian who was in the middle of the crowd if that meant stopping the coup. Suddenly, from the skies, a feathered serpent descended, filling with hope the hearts of the rebels and afraid civilians, the feathered serpent was a sacred symbol in Moon's navel. They used to live in the nation and most of them were eradicated by conquerors. But some of them are still alive, living proof that after all these wars, corruption, and cartels, people of Moon's navel are still standing, fighting.

Quetzalcoatl roared, the center of the city trembled, some civilians ran out of the event, some were trapped, the army ran from left and right to trap the people in front of the presidential palace.

"Very well Quetzi, good luck in your fight, I'll go and give you a hand after I am done with these soldiers, Hannah, jump a few seconds after me," said Shaddai and happily jumped out of Quetzalcoatl, Hannah was hesitating, she didn't like heights.

Shaddai was falling from the sky, the army shot at the crowd, but Carlos defended the right side with a giant mental aura wall; Jorge defended the left side with his magnetic powers stopping the bullets, Shaddai closed his eyes and remember what happened to his family, what happened to Omid, what happened to Juan, to chuck, he thought of everything that was happening in the country, his body started to shine blue.

"Sadness, Sad Time!" Shaddai shouted falling in the middle of the left side of the army and one by one they started to drop unconscious, some even had a heart attack, some of them just fell on their knees to cry, feeling guilty.

Meanwhile, on the other side Carlos dissolved his attack and charged leading the rebellion, Jorge focused on stopping the bullets, Zamudio hit the tanks with explosions, Mike took down some helicopters with a sound wave, Phee and Cupcake pummeled the infantry.

*A country of drugs and bullets*

Hannah jumped and landed after Shaddai, some soldiers were crying but still on their five senses, they shot a special Gatling gun at Shaddai, but Hannah protected him, and punched the soldier to the ground and everyone that was still awake.

"How ya doing?" asked Hannah

"Tired, but not that much, I can still fight," responded Shaddai panting.

Nezahualcoyotl arrived with his forces to support Carlos and the rebels, but he was intercepted by the special forces commanded by general Rodrigo Perez, one of the remaining pillars.

"Seems like we miscalculated the numbers of our enemy," said Nezahualcoyotl.

"We both made the same mistake, 8 sword's army, but you don't have the slightest idea," replied the general.

"I see, you still have an ace under your sleeves, well who said we don't" added the coyote man.

Quetzalcoatl flew straight to the balcony towards the president and left a hole in the palace, Henrick Pine was about to fight Quetzalcoatl inside the Willow house.

## Chapter 32

Gunshots, explosions, screams, the battlefield was cover with them, the Moon's navel army started to fight back, making Nezahualcoyotl's forces stepped back, the rebellion encounter the singular squad, super soldiers that fought against the rebels, Phee used his super strength to punch one of the super-soldiers, Cupcake kicked him on the face assisting Phee.

"Phee! Phee?"

"Don't know but knowing that he is Shaddai's friend he is probably searching for one of the pillars," Cupcake replied and Phee turned around to look for his brother.

Zamudio grabbed one of the super-soldiers by the head and exploded his face, a cannonball was shot aiming at Zamu, but Jorge stopped it and sent it back making an explosion.

## *A country of drugs and bullets*

"You owe me one," said Jorge, and was shot in the back with rubber bullets, Mike created a sound wave that swept all of the rubber bullet snipers.

"And you owe me one," Mike added.

The super soldiers and the snipers eventually managed to corner part of the rebellion, Nezahualcoyotl's men were still being held back by the Special Forces, but Tlaloc came with her men cutting through tanks with her water sword and freezing the infantry and some of the super soldiers. Meanwhile, Shaddai and Hannah were running on the other side of the battlefield.

"We need to go to the Willow house and check on Quetzi," said Shaddai.

"Don't ya trust Quetzi?" said Hannah.

"It's weird that he managed to hit him so easily, either there is a trap inside the presidential palace or Henrick Pine doesn't need to be protected, either way, Quetzi might be in trouble," Shaddai responded.

"Now that I think of it, just as we're searching for the pillars, they must be searching for us, after all, we are symbols of the rebellion," Hannah added.

"You are right, that's what I need back up until I recover, which won't take long," said Shaddai.

Nezahualcoyotl was panting and dropping blood he was receiving a beating, his opponent was Rodrigo Perez, Nezi kicked him and tried to slash him using his machetes.

"Not again," exclaimed Nezi while moving really fast, unable to control his speed, and Rodrigo countered him with a big punch on the face, sending him to the ground.

## *A country of drugs and bullets*

Nezi stood back up and fought, slashing his opponent's Jacket he had 3 lightbulbs on his chests, Nezi was speechless, it was some sort of stoplight, the middle light turned on lighting yellow and everything started to feel slow, Rodrigo dashed launching powerful punches, the coyote man slowly lifted his guard but received another beating making him flinch, he managed to cover most of it and survived.

"You revealed my secret, I am a traffic light man," said Rodrigo.

"What a stupid power," said Nezi panting and bleeding.

"Let's see if that's true," exclaimed Rodrigo and the third light turned on shining red, Nezi couldn't move.

Rodrigo hit his enemy with everything he got, jab, straight, jab, jab, right hook, left uppercut, straight, low kick, right uppercut, left hook, high kick, and one finishing body blow, Nezi fell having difficulties breathing, the general of Moon's navel army was about to stomp Nezi's skull but he was stopped by a green energy blast on the face, the turned around and was cut by Carlos and his green mental aura blade.

"Thank... you," mumbled Nezi.

"Thank me when I beat him, this is going to be hard," said Carlos.

# Chapter 33

Shaddai and Hannah ran towards Willow house, but they were stopped by a brunette woman with curly brown shiny hair in a deep blue dress.

"Wait ain't she the famous soap opera star?" asked Hannah.

"They are called telenovelas, jeez, why do you have to be so white Hannah?" Shaddai replied.

"Anyway, she is Mouette the first lady, and the symbol of this country's largest media company, one of the remaining pillars," Hannah added.

"Well you take care of her, I am going inside to check on Quetzi," Shaddai said and started running.

*A country of drugs and bullets*

"Why? Y'all afraid of fighting a woman?" said Hannah teasing Shaddai.

"Wait a minute, who said you could escape?" Mouette exclaimed.

"I said it!" -Shaddai answered yelling and hitting Mouette in the face and putting her on the ground. - "I leave it to you."

Shaddai ran, Mouette stood up and transformed into a harpie lady, with claws on her feet and white wings instead of hands, she screamed.

"Wait, she transformed? But" thought Hannah concerned, her train of thought was interrupted by the harpie lady.

Meanwhile, at the other side of the battlefield, Carlos was fighting Rodrigo Perez, the general threw a hook, uppercut, and straight blow, Carlos dodged and countered him, then he stepped back and created some distance.

Rodrigo dashed towards him with a tight guard, but Carlos kept his distance, the general's green light on his chest turned on, hypnotizing his opponent, Carlos' movements were accelerated and because of that he was losing control, Rodrigo took the opportunity and stopped Carlos' movements with a cross counter that broke Carlos' helmet.

Carlos was taken down and his face was bleeding, he quickly stood up, his movements were unpredictable due to his opponent's abilities, Carlos started shooting green aura blasts with extreme velocity, Rodrigo blocked them with his arms, but Carlos slashed him.

"Psycho cut."

Rodrigo turned on the next light and Carlos' movements were slowed down, the general closed the distance between them, jab, straight, left uppercut, right hook, left hook, and a kick to the guts, but Carlos glowed with aura and covered his suit with his Ashura mode.

Carlos grabbed Rodrigo by his neck and punched him with one of the upper Ashura's arms, the effect of Rodrigo's powers wore off and Carlos threw a barrage of hits with his 6 Ashura hands. Hundreds of hits landed in Rodrigo's body, but Carlos suddenly stopped, the general turned on the third light, paralyzing Carlos.

"Brace yourself," said Rodrigo, squaring up.

Jab, jab, straight, hook, uppercut, hit with the knee, high kick, straight punch, left low kick, right uppercut, Rodrigo ravaged while his opponent was paralyzed, Ashura started cracking up.

"Oh no, he is almost as strong as Shaddai in Angry mode."

Rodrigo broke Carlos' mental armor but the combination of hits didn't stop, he continued to punch and kick until he broke the suit, Carlos wasn't able to move.

"Huh? What's up? Stand up...seems like I don't need to use my powers anymore, you can't move, you've become a sandbag now."

Rodrigo Perez punched Carlos, hit him several times, and kicked him in the face sending him against some rock. Carlos' body was bleeding a lot, the general was going to finish the job.

"I am used to fighting without being able to move, but, what about you? Do you know how it feels?" Carlos asked scowling, his eyes glowed green, and moved his hands towards Rodrigo paralyzing him.

"What's going on?" said Rodrigo, he was scared, feeling how his muscles tensed and stopped responding.

"I still have my singularity, I still have my mind," said Carlos angry.

Nezahualcoyotl stood up and took one of his machetes and slashed Rodrigo on his chest, Carlos focused his energy and shot a laser beam.

"Psybeam!" Carlos exclaimed.

The beam hit Rodrigo leaving him on the floor unconscious.

"I am sorry, but He is too dangerous, I am going to steal the kill," said Nezi, killing Rodrigo with his machete.

"Seems like we are square," Carlos said, panting.

Nezi took care of Carlos' wounds and then took care of his own injuries, Phee arrived and was astonished after seeing Carlos beat up and the suit he built broken.

"Pheeee!" said Phee running towards his brother.

"I know, sorry but you can fix it right?" Carlos asked his brother.

"Phee," Phee answered.

Shaddai ran and entered the presidential palace and to his surprise it was empty, he took the stairs and went to the upper floors, and then, he saw a Tyrannosaurus Rex with Quetzalcoatl on its jaw, bleeding.

"Excuse me sir, but you are chewing my friend," said Shaddai cracking his knuckles.

## Chapter 34

"I was correct, they had a trap prepared to ambush Quetzi, sorry it took me a while to recover," said Shaddai to Quetzi who was lying on the floor defeated.

"Oh no, I don't need protection, not anymore, thanks to the universal church," said Henrick Pine, turning back into his human form.

"What? But morphers can't transform," exclaimed Shaddai.

"Not natural ones, but artificial morphers with good genes like me can go back to human form," Pine explained.

## *A country of drugs and bullets*

"Well that's good to know, so there is a way to go back huh? Maybe I need to go to the universal church," Shaddai said excitedly, turning into happy mode, glowing yellow, he moved fast in front of Pine and punched him in the face.

"Going against a country is bold enough but getting in the church's business is a suicide, they've been in powers for thousands of years," said Pine spitting blood.

"People in power are always changing, like this country," said Shaddai.

"Why are you doing all this?" asked Pine, turning back into a T rex.

"Because of my friends," said Shaddai excited to fight a talking dinosaur, Pine roared.

"Happy spear" -said Shaddai throwing a jab. - "Happy shotgun, merry bullets," said Shaddai hitting the T rex with a straight punch and more jabs.

Pine tried to bite Shaddai, but he moved to the left and dodged, the dinosaur moved his tail, Shaddai ducked avoiding the hit.

"You are tough, let's try with more solid punches, Happy tomahawk" -Shaddai hit with a left hook. - "Happy bazooka!" Shaddai hit using both of his palms, and the dinosaur flinched.

The T rex hit Shaddai with his tail in his right side breaking his ribs, Shaddai flew away, Pine pursued him, and skull bashed him, sending him to another room breaking a lot of walls.

The president tried to stomp Shaddai, but he disappeared using his speed.

*A country of drugs and bullets*

"Happy Magnums," yelled Shaddai, throwing a one-two on the dinosaur's face, but Pine took him down with a headbutt.

"I am faster, but my punches aren't damaging him enough," Shaddai thought, the T rex tail whipped him and ripped his T-shirt with the hit and sent him to another room on the floor.

"I really liked that T-shirt," said Shaddai, entering angry mode, his muscles swelled and started glowing red.

Henrick Pine dashed towards Shaddai, and skull bashed him.

"Angry Bazooka!" yelled Shaddai and stopped the skull bash sending the dinosaur to another floor, Shaddai pursued him to hit him.

"Angry tomahawk" -Shaddai exclaimed, throwing a right hook, the dinosaur screeched in pain. - "Angry shotgun," Shaddai punched the T rex in the guts but the dinosaur bit Shaddai's right shoulder and threw him away.

Shaddai fell and screamed in pain, leaving a blood trail, the T rex roared, and proceeded to finish the job.

"Damn it, I am now hurting him but I am too slow, like Carlos said, I can't maintain both power-ups at the same time, but maybe I can change from one mode to the other really fast," thought Shaddai dodging the dinosaur's rampage.

Shaddai kept his distance using angry spears, fast and heavy jabs.

"Angry, Happy, Angry, Happy," thought Shaddai, making faces, avoiding tail whips and headbutts.

"Happy mode!" - exclaimed Shaddai laughing and running in circles around Henrick pine- "Happy, Angry, Happy, Angry," yelled Shaddai.

"Angry mode, furious body, angry missile!" shouted Shaddai dashing at full speed towards his opponent hitting him with a right uppercut lifting the T rex through the roofs of the palace. Shaddai jumped.

"That wasn't fast enough, happy, angry, happy, angry, Happy Gatling gun!" thought Shaddai, changing to happy mode and casting a rain of fists into Henrick Pine's body moving through the remaining ceilings of the building until they went through all of them, Shaddai and the T rex were floating in the sky above the building, above the battlefield.

"BIPOLAR BAZOOKA!" yelled Shaddai glowing orange for a moment and hit the president of Moon's navel with everything, the dinosaur went through all the floors hitting the pavement, the impact destroyed the whole palace lifting the rubble, a storm of dust covered the battlefield, and Shaddai fell to the debris from the sky, due to all the dust and impact of the attack, everyone knew something happened, but no one knew the outcome of the fight.

# Chapter 35

While Shaddai was inside Willow house, Hannah was fighting Mouette, the harpie lady avoided all of Hannah's attacks flying, She tried to scratch Hannah's face with her claws but her tough skin protected her, Mouette tried a different strategy, She grabbed Hannah by the shoulders and flew to the skies dropping her. Hannah was afraid of heights and terrified she hit the floor, but she didn't receive much damage, Mouette tried again, she grabbed her and Hannah tried to escape, the harpie lady flew even higher this time and dropped her.

"Oh, dear lord, please help me," Hannah pleaded in her mind. Mouette dove and hit Hannah in the abdomen with her wing increasing the speed of the fall, Hannah grabbed Mouette's wing and didn't let go, the harpie lady tried to fly away but both of them hit the floor leaving a deep hole in the battlefield.

Hannah stood up and squared up remembering Shaddai's training.

"You are strong, but some technique behind your moves will make you unstoppable, look, I'll show you how to throw a straight punch," said Shaddai in Hannah's memories. She stepped firmly, rotated her hips, her power moved through her back moving forward her shoulder and rotating her fist, hardening it. Hannah threw a perfect straight diamond punch directed to Mouette's chin, breaking her jaw.

"Seems like your career is over now," said Hannah winning the fight, but suddenly a huge explosion destroyed the presidential palace, and a big dust cloud covered the center of the navel.

"Shaddai!" yelled Hannah worried.

Nezahualcoyotl, Carlos, and Phee noticed the destruction as well, Phee was busy trying to fix Carlos' suit.

"What do you think happened?" asked Nezahualcoyotl.

"I really doubt Quetzalcoatl lost and knowing Shaddai, I know he went straight to help him, but that's not the problem, people are still fighting, Rodrigo and most likely Henrick pine already lost, maybe all the pillars were taken down, but they army need to know, we need to destroy their morale," Carlos said.

"Phee."

The debris started to shake and suddenly an army of human reptiles, dinosaurs, and deformed hybrids came out of the ruins of the palace, the failed experiments of the universal church and the Moon's navel government were freed attacking everyone, some of them jumped over Hannah biting her.

## *A country of drugs and bullets*

Zamudio, Jorge, Mike, and Cupcake started fighting these artificial morphers, Zamudio exploded the face of a velociraptor, Jorge punched a triceratops on the ribs, Cupcake kicked a lizard man in the head, Mike stopped a brontosaurus with a sound wave.

The field was full of reptile hybrids fighting swordsmen, a Komodo dragon-man spat venom to the rebels, and 8 swords army members killing them. These morphers eventually arrived where Carlos and Nezi were, at the back of the battlefield.

Carlos stopped a few of them with his mental powers, Nezahualcoyotl used his remaining strength to slash through them, teaming up with Carlos but both of them were tired after fighting Rodrigo, an iguana man attacked Nezahualcoyotl, but Phee punched him breaking its skull and saving Nezi.

A Dino man jumped to attack Carlos from his back, Phee wasn't going to be able to protect him, but Tlaloc arrived and froze the dinosaur, saving Carlos, another hybrid attacked Tlaloc, but Carlos shot an aura blast protecting her, everyone was protecting their comrades, but the sheer quantity was enough to make them fall, Carlos was kicked, Tlaloc slashed, Phee was bitten, Nezahualcoyotl stomped.

"Damn it Shaddai what the fucking shit are you doing?" mumbled Carlos and was kicked again in the face by a reptilian.

The rebellion was having troubles as well, the 8 sword's army was moving back, this cheered up the Moon's navel army.

"We can do it, we are going to win!" yelled one of the soldiers of Moon's navel.

"For the navel!" shouted another one, and they started shooting their enemies. Growls, swords clashing, gunshots, roars, hopeless screams, and explosions could be heard throughout the city. Civilians hiding in their homes started praying and suddenly the ground started to shake.

## *A country of drugs and bullets*

"What is that?" said Jorge, punching a soldier.

"It sounds like thousands of steps, like a big march," said Mike.

"It's the caravan of immigrants!" exclaimed Jorge.

"Are... are those the immigrants?" Carlos said lying on the floor.

"No, those aren't just immigrants," said Nezahualcoyotl crying.

"Those are 8 swords army members working under admiral 8, Joao Santos!" exclaimed Tlaloc.

"Listen, everybody, let's help our Moon's navel brothers, fight with all your hearts, fight like this is your own country!" exclaimed Joao, a black muscular man with long dreadlocks tied in a ponytail and a long metallic spear on his right hand.

"For the new continent!" and after a war cry, they charged after the Moon's navel army and their artificial morphers, cutting through all of them. Joao went to help Nezi and Tlaloc.

"Where is Shane?" Joao asked.

"He wasn't able to arrive in time, but he managed to take down Chopo," Tlaloc informed.

"Well, in that case, sorry for the delay," Joao said.

"Wait, we can't just keep fighting and lose lives, after all these people are just fighting to protect the country, they are victims as well in some shape or form," Carlos said, grabbing Joao's leg, stopping him.

"Who is this," asked admiral 8

"The symbol of this rebellion," answered Nezahualcoyotl.

## *A country of drugs and bullets*

"What do you suggest then?" asked Joao.

"Lead them to the palace ruins, keep them close to the ruins until Shaddai or Quetzi come out of the debris," Carlos suggested.

"What if they don't come out?" Joao asked.

"Don't underestimate my friend," Carlos stated firmly, and Joao smiled.

"Listen everyone!" -shouted Joao lifting his spear. - "Let's corner them against the ruins!"

Joao's forces followed Carlos' plan and after, blood, tears, bruises, and sweat they managed to corner the army against the ruins, but time passed and they didn't stop fighting back, and no one came out of the debris.

Hannah punched her way out of the artificial morphers ambush and climbed the pile of debris and started digging, but before she dug any deeper and before the rebellion hesitated. Shaddai came out of the ruins with a body on his left shoulder.

"Listen, everyone! The cartel is dead, your corrupt government has been vanquished, everyone you're fighting for has been defeated," exclaimed Shaddai standing on top of the ruins while the army kept fighting.

"Everyone that has been paying you is either dead or no longer in a position of power to benefit you, we are all fighting for the same thing, for freedom, for prosperity, for a decent life, but we aren't going to achieve that if we don't start fighting together if you don't believe me, I took care of your president myself," said Shaddai and threw Henrick Pine's body to the middle of the fight.

*A country of drugs and bullets*

After hearing Shaddai's words, realizing they were cornered and looking at the president's body and the destroyed palace, one by one, they stopped fighting and surrendered.

"Shaddai!" -Shouted Hannah in tears, she ran after Shaddai. "You won!"

Shaddai sat down tired and bleeding.

"Let me help you," said Hannah worried.

"Hannah, thank you for covering me, thank you for following me in all this mess, you are great," said Shaddai touching her head. Hannah noticed that Shaddai was serious, he wasn't smiling, and he was tired, he wasn't able to use his singularity, Shaddai's words were his honest, true feelings. Everyone was crying with joy or celebrating the end of the battle.

Hannah looked into Shaddai's eyes and blushed, but she didn't stop looking, Shaddai grabbed her and kissed her, the war was over.

## Chapter 36

Quetzalcoatl was hospitalized, as well as Tlaloc, Nezahualcoyotl, and everyone with injuries from the fight, Phee finished fixing and even upgrading Carlos' suit, Shaddai slept for a week, the rebellion started chasing down some corrupt mayors and senators.

Shaddai woke up and Hannah was taking care of him. The first thing Shaddai wanted to do was eat, the country was grateful, so they fed him.

## *A country of drugs and bullets*

"Shaddai, we need to talk," Hannah said after Shaddai was done eating.

"About what happened at the ruins?" Shaddai asked and Hannah punched him.

"No, about the old continent, that's why y'all searched for me, right?"

"Oh, that is correct, you know a lot about it, especially about the sacred texts," Shaddai added.

"Well, not sure about that, but almost every religion and even history point out that the secret of how singularities work is in the old continent, where first humans appeared, but that's about it, there is no historic registry about that or any scientific study," Hannah explained.

"I see, but I suspect that there are some clues inside the sacred texts, and after learning what the universal church can do, I am convinced," said Shaddai.

"That's where it gets tricky, some stories in the sacred texts are regarded as history, some of it is regarded as poetic, symbolic, prophetic, and just theology, what is weird is that there aren't any historical records that prove or disprove any of this," Hannah added.

"Maybe the universal church is hiding the truth," Shaddai said.

"I don't think is that easy, I think the united nations are involved as well, that's why the center of the old continent is always at war, maybe governments want to know the truth and are fighting to unveil it, but maybe they are fighting to hide it, that's why it is unclear what parts of the secret texts are facts and what parts are symbolic, I mean the universal church's version of the sacred texts include more books, and I believe those are fake to maintain people skeptical," Hannah said while taking a cup of tea to relax, Shaddai remained silent for a moment, thinking.

## *A country of drugs and bullets*

"That's why I didn't want to follow you, look at all this mess just for finding me, I know that if you go to the old continent, you are going to learn the truth of this world and challenge some fearsome people, provoking a lot of chaos, and that's being optimistic, maybe you just die at the hands of the people in power, Shaddai, I won't stop you, so if you want to go, the countries of Ammi and Loammi are the key to all of this," Hannah said and took a sip of tea. Shaddai laughed and tried to relax with Hannah, knowing she was worried.

Some days passed and Quetzalcoatl and his friends said goodbye to Shaddai and his friends.

"Thanks for helping us guys, but we need to follow with our agenda, I hope I can see you again and maybe in more peaceful times," said Quetzi.

"Thanks for giving us a trip through the skies Quetzi," said Shaddai.

"You know what...is growing on me," said Quetzi.

"Eh... thank you for saving Nezi and for helping in the battle, you were great," said Tlaloc to Carlos.

"Don't sweat it," said Carlos, and Tlaloc left with her friends.

Quetzi's gang traveled with Joao's forces in order to find Shane.

The rebels formed an alliance to protect the country, after a few days, an assembly took place in order to find the next leader of the nation, Shaddai, Carlos, and Hannah attended the meeting and they even nominated Shaddai to be the leader.

"I am the worst person to be a president, and besides I am not even from this country," said Shaddai, rejecting the position.

## *A country of drugs and bullets*

Some nominated Carlos, due to his skills and character shown on the battlefield, but Carlos refused as well.

"I promised to follow Shaddai on his adventure, and after all this, I can say it is going to get way more interesting than being a president," said Carlos

"Perhaps we can help with that," said a tall black man with a blue suit followed by 2 even bigger men. Everyone was astonished.

"It's Beracah! The president of Eagle nest!" said Hannah terrified, thinking he was after Shaddai and her. Everyone got worried.

"Do not worry, we came in order to help our neighbor in need," exclaimed president Beracah with a huge smile.

They didn't want eagle nest to interfere in their political process, but they were afraid of being too rude against the leader of one of the most powerful nations.

"I see what your concern is, I promise, Eagle nest won't get involved in the choosing of your new leader, for now, I only want to help by rebuilding the Navel and the presidential palace."

After a few negotiations, everyone left except for Beracah, his men, Shaddai, Hannah and Carlos.

"Very well Shaddai, Hannah, Great job!" said the president leaving Shaddai and his friends confused.

"You brought freedom to this country and fought the cartel, which was an enemy of ours, congratulations, because of that we want to offer you a special position in our army," added Beracah.

"Ha! Sorry sir, but I am not interested in becoming a soldier, I have some stuff to do, your only concern is that we aren't perceived as

## *A country of drugs and bullets*

terrorists, to avoid conflicts in the United Nations," said Shaddai daringly.

"You should show more respect, brat!" scolded one of Beracah's men, a tall guy with spiky hair and pointy teeth.

"Shaddai! Shut up, don't you know who they are? David Eagle the general of the aerial forces and Erick Shark, Admiral of the marines, together with John Whale and Kevin Bull lead the strongest army in the world, we are no match for them," said Hannah.

"At least one of them is educated," said David Eagle, a blond well-trimmed man.

"I know I can't beat them in a fight, but if they kill us, Moon's navel will complain at the United Nations meeting. There is a lot of tension between the countries right now, people are already assuming the worst of you because of what happened here," said Shaddai.

"Sir, permission to kill him," asked Erick Shark.

"No, no, he is only speaking his mind freely, and that's the spirit of our country, freedom of speech, right? And besides, he is right, we do not want problems with anyone and what you guys did may trigger some international leaders, but make no mistake, we can kill you, we only have to report you first at the united nations as terrorists and take care of that ourselves, even if Moon's navel interfere, but that route is a waste of potential, we think that we can work together and make you heroes," said Beracah charmingly.

"Also, we do not want you as a soldier, we want you as a symbol, just a special relationship between you guys and the army," added David Eagle.

"Well, that's not entirely true, one mission, we want you to work in one mission only, you are perfect for it, and we know a lot

## *A country of drugs and bullets*

about you, we know you are interested in the religion of the living God, so this mission might interest you," said Beracah.

Shaddai was silently looking at Carlos and what this might imply.

"What do you mean? What kind of mission and what about my friend?"

"The old continent, we want you to be in one special mission in the war between Ammi and Loammi, your passion and power, might help our troops to solve this conflict but doesn't matter what happens, after the mission you will be free of doing pretty much what you want, and about your friend, well we can help with his migration process and speed it up, but only if he is willing to," said the Eagle nest leader. All of them were left surprised by the proposition.

"We should wait for Quetzi and the gang, we can travel with them," said Shaddai, not wanting to go back to Eagle nest.

"This might be for the best, if we go with Quetzi maybe we can be safe but we are going to be tagged as terrorists, this way we can do our own lives," persuaded Hannah.

"I am with Hannah in this one, we can't go around the world making enemies of everyone, and besides they are taking us to our destination," added Carlos.

Shaddai thought about it and having the safety and peace of his friends in mind, he decided to work with the Eagle nest's government, they shook hands and made the deal.

"Very well then, let's go back home and then to the old continent," said Shaddai.

Manufactured by Amazon.ca
Bolton, ON